—Contents—

Part One — 1916

Becoming a Woman   1

Part Two — 1930

Baby   9

Concubine   24

The Most Beautiful Girl in the Village   36

Letter to My Daughter   47

Part Three — 1940

Deaths in the Family   57

The Good Luck Girl   68

A Low, Wet Room   76

The Red Skirt   85

Part Four — 1950

Big Feet   99

Part Five — 1964

Saving Nu Shu   119

—

Afterword   133

Sewing the Story   143

Acknowledgements   145

Glossary   147

Bibliography   153

LONELY RIVER VILLAGE

VILLAGE
A Novel of Secret Stories

Norma Libman

This is a work of fiction. It is based on writings of unknown women who told their stories in the secret Nu Shu script of the Hunan Province in pre-Communist China.

RGP
RIO GRANATA PRESS

Cover illustration and book design
Gary W. Priester
Author Photo: Mary E. Carter

For my wonderful children,
Dan and Molly, Amy and Joseph,
and Marc and Christina, and my amazing
grandchildren Benny and Madeleine, Miya, Rose
and Oscar, and Miles.

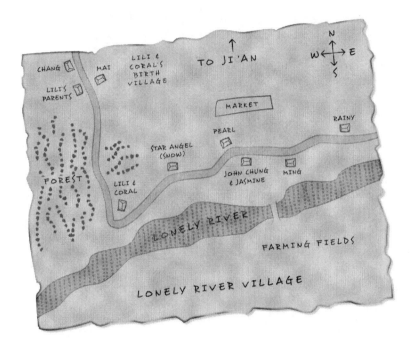

"Effortless, lyrical, passionate, heartbreaking, transformative. A beautiful, powerful and potent story. A moving and dramatic tale that's also based in history."
—Aurin Squire, journalist, essayist, playwright at Royal Academy of Dramatic Art, Greater New York City Area
Oboma-ology Juilliard New Play Festival 2014 and Fenburgh Theatre in London 2014 • *To Whom it May Concern* Abingdon Theatre and Arc Light Theatre in New York

"Reading this book is a sheer joy. Norma Libman recounts these stories in a style as hauntingly lovely as the embroidered writing of the Nu Shu in which they were recorded. This should be required reading for all women, especially young women whose lives are lived with openness, joy, and the blessings of freedom to learn, grow, and determine their own destinies."
—Paula Amar Schwartz, award-winning psychologist and poet.
Beyond Time and Space, Unfolding Universe

". . . clear, concise, spare, and poetically evocative, giving the impression of a whispered confidence. The minimalist style of disclosure fit the book's intention and the characters themselves. I felt empathy for these unfortunate women . . . [and] grateful for the vastly more privileged life I have been born into."
—New Mexico Press Women Communications Contest

RIO GRANATA PRESS

PART ONE — 1916

— PART ONE - 1916 —

BECOMING A WOMAN

*"If women's tears were gathered
they would make a river wider
and longer than the Yangtze River."*
—Anonymous Nu Shu

It was almost midnight and Blossom had just finished sewing the binding cloths for her daughter Lili's feet. She had put off starting the foot binding process until Lili was almost seven years old. She had heard rumors that foot binding was now illegal in China but she didn't believe it. Neither did anyone else she knew, and everyone was still binding their daughters' feet. She knew that now she really needed to begin and her plan was to start the next morning. Blossom looked at the cloth – red for good luck, and to dull the shock of the blood, too. Maybe it will not frighten Lili so much when she sees blood on her feet for the first time, she thought. Maybe it will not look so ugly against the red of the cloth as it would on some other color.

Blossom remembered the first time she saw blood on her own binding cloths, when her own mother was working so diligently to make her feet beautiful. She was terrified. She knew that foot binding was important and painful. But blood. She had never envisioned blood, and she was sure Lili had not either. So she decided – back when Lili was a toddler, just learning to walk – to use red cloth so the contrast would not be so stark.

The sun was as bright as could be the next morning, blasting through the windows with a vengeance and making the metal table in the kitchen shine in the children's eyes as they ate breakfast. The two boys wolfed down their food and followed their father – waiting impatiently – out to the fields. Only little Lili lingered over her food, maybe picking up a feeling from her anxious mother, maybe sensing that something was going to happen this morning.

When Lili put her chopsticks down beside her rice bowl, Blossom scooped her up from her chair and held her close. So tight that Lili's little six-year-old body squirmed in her mother's arms.

"It's time, Lili," Blossom said. "We're going to start your feet this morning. We're going to turn you into a beautiful woman."

Lili felt a rush of excitement and fear, so closely mixed together she couldn't separate the two emotions.

"My feet, Mama?" she said. "Oh, no. Not yet. Please. I'm afraid."

Lili had no older sisters so she had not seen the process first hand. But she was already learning Nu Shu, the women's secret writing, with her sworn sisters, her best friends. Two of them had

had their feet bound and the others had watched their sisters go through it. They all knew it hurt. Some had cried. Others had been brave and choked back the tears. But they all had been in pain and everyone knew it. One girl even told the story of a cousin who had died from infections in her feet because her mother had not kept the binding cloths clean enough.

A wave of fear gripped Lili and she circled her arms around her mother's neck. Her arms were strong and she held on tight but her stomach was weak. It churned and churned and Lili felt that she might lose her breakfast.

Blossom loosened Lili's arms and set the child down on the edge of the kitchen table.

"We must do this, Lili, if you are to become a beautiful woman and find a husband. If you don't marry, your brothers will have to take care of you for all of your life and they will not like that. And you will never have children of your own if you don't marry. Come now, we will start today. It will not hurt so much if you are a brave girl."

Blossom kept Lili sitting on the kitchen table and removed the soft slippers she wore in the house. She looked at her daughter's perfect little six-year-old feet and wished she didn't have to bind them so tight that the bones would break, wished the two of them could just go over to the fireplace and sew together all morning. She hated to make her child cry, but there were no choices here. Blossom had lived through it and Lili would too.

First Blossom took a clean rag and soaked it in warm, soapy

water. Then she washed Lili's feet gently and carefully, taking special care to clean between the toes where infection could start early on in the process. Finally she reached into the pocket of her apron and pulled out the red binding cloths.

"Look, Lili. I've sewn them just for you. They wish you beauty and happiness all your life. Can you read the Nu Shu?"

Lili might have been able to read the symbols if only she could have seen them clearly. But when she tried, they all began to move on the red cloth, swimming in a watery haze of her own tears, which she was desperately trying to keep from rolling down her cheeks.

But at last the tears freed themselves and Lili cried and begged her mother to wait just one more day. Blossom took Lili's feet and quickly wrapped each one in a red cloth. She didn't make the cloth too tight. There would be plenty of time for that the next day. This was just to get Lili used to the idea that the cloths would be on her feet for at least part of every day for the rest of her life. That's what Blossom hoped. She didn't want Lili to turn into one of those women who unwrapped their feet after they were married, but she knew she would have no control over that.

The next day Lili sat quietly on the edge of the table while her mother washed her feet and wrapped them – a little bit tighter than the day before. And the next day, tighter still. After the feet were wrapped Lili was made to walk. Every day it became more and more difficult to walk. More painful. Harder to keep her balance. The pain shot up through her arches, through her calves, up her thighs and into her hips. All she wanted to do was lie down but Blossom would not let her stop until she walked from the kitchen to the bedroom two times, every day. Sometimes Lili cried. Sometimes Blossom turned her head so Lili would not see the tears filling her own eyes.

"Like this," Blossom would say, and she would demonstrate the walk for Lili. As if Lili had not seen her mother walk every day of her young life.

Sometimes Lili would lose her balance and fall. It happened often in the beginning. It felt so strange to walk with her feet so cramped in her tiny shoes. As her feet grew, her bones broke, one after another, every time with a new wave of pain, and each foot settled into its new shape, both almost exactly the same but not quite. Only Lili could notice the slight difference between them.

Every night Blossom would unwrap Lili's feet and wash them again. She would sigh with relief when there was no smell of rotting flesh that would signify the start of an infection. She would look at the bottom of each foot to see how much like a lotus flower it was beginning to look. She handled the tiny broken bones as carefully as she could. After some months they began to look right to her. And Lili's walking got better. The pain subsided. She smiled again sometimes. When Lili smiled, Blossom smiled.

Lili was seven years old by this time and ever so much more worldly. She liked the way her feet looked. She comforted her friends when they began their foot binding. She thanked her mother for making her a beautiful woman.

Blossom and Lili became closer than ever. Lili loved her father and she loved her two brothers. But when it was time for her to be married out and move two miles away to Lonely River, where her new husband's family lived, it was her mother she missed the most.

She longed for her mother to be with her when she had her own children. But Blossom could never leave her duties at home. Lili's husband's family never wanted to spare her from her chores so she could go back to see her mother. In fact, it was ten years from the time of her marriage until Lili was able to find a way to make a trip home. When she did, she found that nothing was as she had left it.

PART TWO — 1930

— PART TWO - 1930—

BABY

"I find some relief in writing
for one cannot always cry."
—Anonymous Nu Shu

The last thing Lili expects to do this sunny day is take a two mile walk. She is comfy sitting on the edge of her bed and staring at her precious feet. They are the feet that have earned her a place in one of the best homes in Lonely River, a village in the Hunan Province of China. But they are not likely to carry her far from home because she can barely balance on them and when she does stand for more than a few minutes they begin to cause pain that starts at her toes and slowly travels all the way up to her hips.

Her feet are little more than three inches long, having been bound and broken so perfectly by her mother when Lili was six years old that the soles, all bent and curled up on themselves, resemble a lotus flower. It is not because of her lustrous black hair or smooth skin, but because her feet are so beautiful in the eyes of men that Lili was married to one of the richest, most important men in the village. And because she continued to keep her feet bound – did not loosen the cloths that wrapped them tightly at night as some women did once they had snagged a good husband – that she has been married now for ten years. And not cast aside, either, when a concubine joined the family two years ago.

Lili lets her eyes move slowly around the room, her own bedroom, that she occupies on the nights her husband does not call her into his room. She sees the elegant wooden dresser with the silver handles on the doors, carved with what she always imagines are scenes from life in the imperial palace. The curtains on the windows are of the finest brocade, colored in vivid reds and yellows. Even the chamber pot is beautiful to her eye. It has been painted by a fine artist with scenes of children picnicking in the lush Chinese countryside.

And at the foot of the bed is her favorite item of all: a huge travel trunk, exquisitely carved also, with a clasp as big as Lili's fist. Folded on the chest is a beautiful bed cover, embroidered by Lili herself. The symbols she sewed around the edges hold a secret. They are not just a pretty design. They are Nu Shu, the secret writing of the women of Hunan Province. They form a story that tells some of the events of Lili's life. But they can only be interpreted by women who know the code. To Lili's husband, for instance, they are no more than pretty pictures.

Today is Lili's mother's birthday and Lili wants nothing more than to visit her mother and bring her a gift, especially because her mother is forty now, and Lili has not seen her in the ten years she has been married. She worries that her mother may have changed much, have white hair, perhaps, and wrinkly skin. Lili has asked her husband's permission to visit her mother this day and he has denied her. As he has every other time she has asked. He will not provide a carriage to take her and she does not see how she can possibly walk the two miles alone on her tiny, bound feet.

After nearly ten years of living in her husband's wealthy family home Lili still feels out of place. She has given them the sons they required of her and fulfilled her obligations to her mother-in-law with good grace, according to Chinese custom of the time, but she has never really felt part of the family. Far from it. They have let her know at every possible moment that she is not one of them. That she never will be.

Lili's own family is poor. Her mother-in-law reminds her often of her great good luck in marrying into such a well-established, revered, financially comfortable family. Her mother-in-law tells Lili that she doesn't work as hard as she should to show her thankfulness for her good luck. Her husband doesn't care how she feels, doesn't know how she feels. Hers was an arranged marriage as were those of all her dear girlfriends, her sworn sisters, with whom she grew up. The girlfriends still love each other deeply. For most of them, their husbands are just the men whose families they now live with. Lili and her husband rarely speak to one another. She obeys him, as she does his mother, and stays out of trouble as best she can.

Again Lili looks down at her feet. Despite the lowness of her own family and the poor dowry they offered, Lili was wanted by several men because of her tiny, beautiful feet. She was a lucky girl to have had a mother who took such care to break the bones in her feet properly so each little foot would slowly form itself into the likeness of a perfect lotus flower, the shape that men covet to look at, to fondle and to provide them exquisite sexual satisfaction. Because of her mother's diligent work when Lili was only six, Lili was betrothed into a wealthy family by the time she was eight and a certain status came to her first family because of it. Not money. But some measure of status that was more than they would have had if not for Lili's tiny feet.

But when she looks at her feet Lili does not see them as valuable treasures anymore. Now she sees something different: a trap. Lili can walk about and bring her mother-in-law tea. She can do the laundry; she can clean the bedpans. She can service her husband in bed at his command. But she cannot go anywhere. She cannot walk far on her tiny feet without experiencing a searing pain. And Lili wants to walk. She wants to walk to her family home and bring her mother a birthday present, maybe even something extra for the family since they are so poor and do without so much. And her husband's family has plenty to spare.

So Lili decides that this is the day she will walk to her mother's house. Now, while it is still early in the morning, she will find a present for her mother and bring it to her. And since her husband will not provide a carriage she will walk. And she will survive the pain because it is something she wants so much to do. She may never have a better opportunity, she knows, because her husband is taking her sons away for the day and she will not be much missed. There is food prepared that her mother-in-law and father-in-law can eat. Even if she dies of the pain in her feet, or from hunger or thirst, she will first see her mother and her old village. And she will give her mother a birthday present.

Lili slides off her bed and stands on her tiny feet, finding her balance carefully before taking a step. She walks out of her bedroom and through the main room of the house where her mother-in-law dozes by the fire. The old woman stirs a bit and Lili pauses; this could be the end of her plans, but no, the woman is still asleep. Out the door, Lili breathes a sigh of relief, a quiet sigh, and begins to walk toward the forest just behind the house. It is to this small but dense forest that Lili has often crept when she needed to seek refuge from the pressures of her husband's family, so she knows the area well. She walks about the edge of the forest, snapping off small, low-hanging branches from the trees and gathering them in her apron. When the pile begins to feel heavy she heads back out of the forest and toward the main part of the village.

Lili knows her apron will be dirty when she arrives at her mother's house. She looks down at all her clothes. They are so ragged and patched you would think to look at her that she was from a very poor family. The real reason they look so poor is that when everyone else in her husband's family gets new clothes she gets only pieces of cloth with which to patch her old clothes. And on New Year's Day, when everyone takes a bath before the big town celebration, she is last and must use the water everyone else has bathed in. So no matter how she tries she never feels really clean, never smells clean either.

Her mother-in-law has set the tone for her treatment, which makes Lili miss her own mother all the more. Lili knows for certain that when her brothers take wives her mother would never be so cruel to them. For all she knows, her brothers have married already and Lili longs with all her heart to see them again and find out what they are doing.

The center of Lonely River, with its few small stores and one teahouse is about a half mile from the forest but it takes almost an hour for Lili to cover the distance. At first she is not in pain, but by the time she gets to where she can see the stores her toes are hurting and the sides of her feet, where normally there would have been strong arches had her feet not been bound, have begun to feel like little arrows are reaching up from the ground and stabbing her. Soon, Lili knows, the pain will begin to travel high up into her legs. And she has still to sell the wood she collected, use the money to buy something for her mother, and walk the remaining distance to her childhood village. And then, somehow, she must also get back home before dark or her disappearance will come to the attention of everyone.

Lili is lucky and sells her wood for forty copper coins to the woman who owns the noodle shop. Then she buys a pound of noodles from the shopkeeper and this is to be the present for her mother. It will be a welcome gift for the whole family and does not weigh so much that it will be a terrible burden for Lili to carry. Still, her feet hurt more with every step as she returns to the path and makes her way to her childhood home.

Lili feels deep inside herself how much she misses her mother and the village she grew up in. Not so far away, really, little more than a mile now. For one with larger feet the walk would be easy. Lili thinks now she is sorry that she did not unwrap her feet every night like some wives do, so they would spread out a bit and get a little bigger and stronger. Now that she is married it wouldn't matter because she can never marry again, even if her husband dies. It is frowned upon in her rural little corner of China. Elsewhere in the world, even in other parts of her own country, changes are happening. Last year in the village square people were saying that foot binding is now outlawed in China. But Lili does not believe it. If she had a daughter, she knows she would bind her feet. How else could she be sure that the child would find a husband? And how could she possibly live without one? Lili will always be afraid to unwrap her own feet – afraid that her husband would notice and beat her. He does love her little lotus feet. Not her, but her feet.

As Lili walks along, she scratches at her scalp now and then. She has some bits of dried blood in her short, black hair that she is not even aware of. Earlier that morning her mother-in-law complained that she was not doing her work quickly enough and her father-in-law grabbed the fire poker and struck her in the head with it. She was dizzy and fell to the floor and the beating stopped at once. "Go easy," her mother-in-law said, "we do not want to have to spend money to replace her."

Lili thinks of other beatings she has had while living with her husband's family. Once they did not give her any food for a whole day, not even a sip of tea. But still she had to do all her work. The next morning she was so hungry she stole a turnip from the food that was meant to feed the pig. When her father-in-law saw that the turnip was missing he knew she took it, and so he had another excuse to attack her. Another time when she had not been fed he pushed her into the latrine because she was not working quickly enough.

She has never traveled this road alone. Twice when she was a small child her father had brought her on short trips of a business nature, but she rode in a wagon then and had no real sense of the distance. Still, Lili knows it is not so far that it can't be walked because her brothers had done it daily when they went to school. As she trudges along the road with careful steps she notices the flowers and the birds and tries not to notice her painful feet. She concentrates instead on how excited her mother will be to see her and wonders how the family home will look after all this time. She takes heart that she has heard no news of deaths or illnesses in her family in the ten years she has been married.

The walk feels longer than Lili expected, but she knows she is going the right way because there is only one road between the two villages. Soon she sees the familiar shape of her childhood village in the distance. She notices too that the sun is very much in her eyes now as it lowers in the western sky, and her brow begins to wrinkle as she tries to calculate how much time she has if she is to return before dark. She will certainly be missed at dinner but all is prepared and with her sons and husband away his parents will think she does not want to take a meal with them and will not mind eating without her. They will walk away from the table when they are finished and will just leave the cleanup for her. But if she is not back before dark, there will be trouble for sure, as that is behavior that would besmirch the reputation of the whole family.

At last Lili sees her own home in the distance. In her heart she is ready to break into a run. She is only twenty-four. She weighs barely one hundred pounds. She is carrying merely a small package. But she cannot run and she knows it. Her heart leaps out ahead of her and by the time she reaches her home, her father and one of her brothers are standing in the doorway, smiling and crying, pulled to the door by a feeling so strong it can only mean that Lili's heart had reached them first and alerted them that she was coming down the path. In her father's arms is a beautiful little girl, no more that two years old.

The reunion is all hugs and kisses and calling out to cousins and dear old friends of the family. But where is her mother? And whose baby is in her father's arms? Lili forgets the pain she has been suffering as she is led to a chair in the kitchen, where meals are taken. The room is as plain as it ever was, with simple wooden chairs around the old metal table that used to shine in her eyes when she ate breakfast on sunny mornings, and the same old stove that was serving the family when Lili lived there. The excitement fades away as everyone else wanders off and she is looking at her brother and father and the baby is put down on the floor. Her father begins to cry, and her brother, she realizes, is looking somber. And still her mother does not come out of the bedroom, nor in through the front door. The little girl walks over to Lili and lifts her arms in an age-old signal to be picked up. So Lili lifts the child into her lap and looks at the two men.

"Older brother has married," her father says. "He and his wife are away visiting her parents, but they live here. Younger brother will marry soon. We have a crowded house, but for me it is a lonely one. This baby is sweet, but your mother died giving birth to her, an unexpected baby, and it has been difficult to take care of her. Soon there will be more babies, from my daughters-in-law. I don't know how I will find a dowry for this little one. I don't know how I can continue to take care of her."

Lili looks at her father and seems to be listening to his words, but all she really hears is "your mother died giving birth to her." "Your mother died." "Your mother died." She hears it over and over, though he only said it once. It does not make any sense at all. She still expects to see her mother walk through the door, the mother who bound her feet so carefully, even as the horrible words are echoing in her head.

Lili picks up the noodles that were to be her mother's present. She has not had a mother for two years and she didn't even know it. How can that be? Lili wonders. She takes the noodles to the stove and begins to cook them. Who would have made this meal if I had not come home? she asks herself. Lili's father brings in a chicken he has killed that morning and she cleans it and cooks it with the noodles. The little girl is sweet; she tugs at Lili's skirt, begging to be picked up again. This is my sister, thinks Lili, my dear sister who is a stranger to me. Who will teach her the secret Nu Shu language of the women? Who will bind her feet? If only some of my old friends still lived in the village and could have told me about my mother's death, Lili thought, by sending me a fan or handkerchief embroidered in Nu Shu. But there was no one left to do that. They have all been married out to men who live in other villages.

The dinner is solemn. As happy as they all were to see Lili, now they are feeling sad because she is so stricken by the news of her mother's death. And worried about her little sister, whose name she has not even learned, whose fate she cannot imagine without dread. "What is the little girl's name?" Lili asks her father.

"I call her Sad Coral. Coral because her complexion was ruddy when she was born. And Sad because what kind of life will she have with no mother to guide her?"

"Father," Lili says, "should I take Sad Coral home with me? I would love to have her with me now that my boys are getting older and spending more time with their father. The family will not want her, of course, because she is a girl, but if I promise to teach her to work obediently she could be a help to me and to them. Maybe they will let me."

Her father laughs at this. Take on another girl, who isn't even their own? What family would want that? "Maybe if she could be a concubine for your husband in ten years," he said. "Otherwise I can hardly believe they would take her."

"No," Lili says. "Not for that. But I want to try. I want to bring her back with me."

"I would be happy to see her go because I cannot afford her," her father says, "but don't be surprised if they will not keep her. You will have a tough fight on your hands." He glances out the window at the darkening night. "And you will already be in trouble when you get home because it will be fully dark by the time you get there. I can take you and Sad Coral in the wagon, but still you are too late."

Lili looks out at the night sky and gasps. In all the commotion she has forgotten the time. Her father says, stay the night, but Lili says, no, that will make it worse. So they decide to go in her father's wagon, just like in old times, Lili next to her father, but now with Sad Coral on her lap.

Lili is light-headed as she slides into the seat beside her father. Her brother hands the little girl up for Lili to put on her lap. The few clothes the child has are tossed in the back of the wagon. Every part of Lili's body aches from the effort she has made today, and from the various beatings she has endured in the past. As they move down the road, the child falls asleep and Lili dozes, too, halfway dreaming of what will happen when she gets home and what has happened in the past when she has done something the family did not approve of. Or even something that wasn't her fault. Like the time she happened accidentally to see her father-in-law bury some gold and silver beneath a rock that was under an old tree. When he saw her standing there he threatened to kill her. He said she was an outsider and should not know a secret about the family. He waved his shovel in her face and she swore she would never tell. He spared her that time, maybe again because he was thinking of the cost of a new wife. What would they all do when she arrived with another mouth to feed?

As they approach the house, Lili awakes and tells her father not to come in with her. She does not want him to see how nice the house is when she only brought noodles for a gift. And she would never want him to know what it cost her in pain to get those noodles; she tries her best to look cheerful and hide her exhaustion.

So Lili says goodnight to her father and leaves the wagon with the sleeping child on one arm and the child's meager wardrobe in her other. Her father places gentle kisses on the foreheads of both his daughters, one a married woman, one still a baby. It is dark and there is not a moon this night to shed even a little light. When she walks through the door her father-in-law is waiting. He is angry because she is late, but he is so surprised by the sleeping baby in Lili's arms that he is speechless. She sets the packet of clothes on the floor and explains as quickly as she can that her mother has died and the little girl is her baby sister. She begs him to let her keep the child and promises that she will teach her to work, that she will be worth the expense of feeding her.

Her father-in-law says, "Put the baby down on the floor," and she does.

Sad Coral stretches and sighs but continues to sleep. And then her father-in-law hits Lili with the palm of his hand across her face. Lili does not move. She is too tired and she knows she has broken the rule of being inside the house before dark and must expect to be punished. He hits her once more and steps away.

"You may keep the little girl if you can teach her to work," he says. "If she is not a good worker we can sell her in a year or two so it will not be a total loss. I do this for you because I have a heart and I know you mourn the loss of your mother."

He turns and walks away. Lili picks up the baby, still sleeping, and, forgetting the dinner dishes, which she will have to clean up in the morning, carries the child to her room along with the packet of clothing. She settles the baby into a corner of her bed and, as much as she would like to just drop into the bed herself and go to sleep, she does not. Instead she takes up her embroidery. She is dizzy from the long day of walking and the raw emotion of losing her mother and finding a sister all at the same time. But she does what she always does at the end of the day, whether it has been easy or hard, happy or sad. She tells the story of her day in the secret women's writing she learned as a child, the Nu Shu script. She sews the symbols of her story into the fabric she holds in her hands.

This act of sewing her thoughts brings some comfort. She feels gratitude to her mother and her aunts and sworn sisters for teaching her the script when she was a little girl. She realizes that now she has her own little girl and the obligation to teach her the Nu Shu so that when she is married she will have comfort when times are tough. She is embroidering a tablecloth to send to a friend who has married a man from another village. She knows it will look beautiful on the table, but it will also tell her friend the story of this day – and many other days – the good moments and the bad.

But on this night her hands are shaking so that she can hardly hold her needle. And her stitches are not as even as she would like to see them. Sometimes she forgets what a certain character is supposed to look like so she has to pause and think hard about what it is she wants to say. Everything she is trying to tell seems to be coming very slowly. Her eyelids flutter several times as if she is going to fall asleep but she forces herself to stay awake. She must finish the story of her day. She never goes to sleep at night without telling her story, without telling her feelings.

She sews long into the night, inscribing her secret voice into this gift, growing more and more tired but not wanting to stop until it is finished. The baby stirs beside her but does not wake up. The last words she sews are, "I hope when you read my embroidery you can understand what I am trying to tell you because my stitch is getting weak. I am so tired."

CONCUBINE

"Lavender bamboo weeps beside the river.
I wash my clothes beside the river and lean against
a rock in the shade of the purple bamboo.
Everybody thinks I am hard working when I wash
clothes, but I am dreaming."
—Anonymous Nu Shu

Star Angel is a concubine. She lives in a home that has, besides the husband, two other concubines, a wife, a mother-in-law and seven children, three belonging to the wife and two each to the other concubines. She has been there for one year and is not with child yet so it is possible they may make her leave and she knows that. They could put her out in the street or send her back to her family. Either fate would be a disgrace so every night when she goes to bed and every morning when she wakes up she prays that the gods will favor her with a child. A boy, of course.

The family would tolerate a girl. It would mean that she had at least tried and it would buy her some time. But it would be an added expense with no great return except household help. A boy would be perfect. She would never have to fear being thrown out if she produced at least one boy who would strengthen the family and carry with him the hope for more.

Star Angel and her family live on the side of the village with the better families. The side where people have more money and the homes are nicer. And every house has some concubines, so there are always women to talk to in the market and when they are at the river washing clothes or outside watching the children. They understand each other. Some of the wives are nice too, and Star Angel would not say that she could complain about her life much. She is not beaten and her mistress protects her from her mother-in-law when necessary. Actually that happens quite often since the mother-in-law does not like Star Angel because she has a crossed eye, her left eye, and truth to tell she is very plain with hair that is never shiny and skin that is not quite milky-white like the other women. Her mother-in-law mutters all the time that if Star Angel does have a baby it might have a crossed eye too and so be worthless to the family. She does not understand why that would be but since the mother-in-law believes it, Star Angel sort of believes it too. But the mother-in-law never hits her and for this Star Angel is grateful.

When she came into this family her mistress, Snow, and the other two concubines all sewed in the evening when their work was done. Star Angel had trouble sewing because of her eye. They have been trying to teach her the symbols they sew, which have the secret code worked into them, but she's not especially good at it. She tries to learn because she wants them to like her and she wants to know the code so she can understand what they are sewing, but it is hard with her eye the way it is. Snow is sweet and patient, almost as though she were Star Angel's own mother, so she wants to please her and will never stop trying to learn.

Snow told her that when her husband brought the first concubine to her home she was angry. She cried for many days and her mother-in-law said, "Why do you cry? It is the way of men. You are too old now and you are losing your beauty. You have two sons. This is much more than many women have." Snow was nineteen then and her position was secure in the family because of her sons but still she was jealous of the concubine. She admitted that to Star Angel.

To be fair to Snow's husband, he is a kind man. He visits all of his concubines on a regular schedule, and his wife, too. He is a good man, well-meaning, and he never beats any of them. And Snow has two sons and only needs to keep them well so they grow up strong. That is what will keep her place in the family safe. If only she knew that her own place was secure, Star Angel thinks. But this can never be until she has a son, a strong, tall son with perfectly straight eyes.

Star Angel does have something special, though. She has the smallest feet of any woman in this family. Her eyes may be crooked and she may even be barren, but her master loves her feet and that will make it difficult for him to part with her. Even his mother, Star Angel hopes, cannot make him do that against his will. He is mad for her feet. When it is her turn to spend the night with him he wants nothing of her but her feet. She could ignore every part of her night time preparations – she doesn't of course – and come to him without painting her face or wearing the proper gown and he would not even notice.

He takes her feet in his hands at once. He devours them with his eyes. He traces with his fingers the folds that make the lotus shape. Her tiny feet give him pleasure. Sometimes he screams with pleasure so that the whole house must hear, but he doesn't care. No, she is safe here as long as she binds her feet tight at all times, unless, well, unless another concubine with tiny feet who is able to conceive a boy comes along. But she tries not to think of that. It is too terrifying.

She enjoys her time with her master. He tires her but she enjoys it. Some concubines hate their masters and often with good reason. If her master ever hit her, she thinks, she would hate him, too. But he does not. He is kind, really, and he does not have to be. He would have the use of her feet no matter how he treated her so it is not necessary to be kind. But he is a good man and all of the women of this house agree on that.

Star Angel's best friend in all the world became a concubine too. It is funny that they both had the same fate as they are different in so many ways. Her friend was the most beautiful girl in the village and Star Angel is plain, but for her feet. Her friend's name is Mai and she was not given as a concubine until several years after Star Angel was. Her father was canny and held out for the best deal he could get, in terms of gifts from prospective suitors. And she became a concubine to a high official in the provincial capital. She was taken away in the grandest carriage and everyone came out to see her being driven off. Star Angel wonders every day what Mai's life is like. She must be in a very grand house, she thinks. It was said that her brothers would achieve high positions because of their connection, through their sister, to this high official but, as far as she knows, this hasn't happened yet. Star Angel would give anything to know how Mai lives her life day to day, what she eats, what clothes and jewels she has now. She hopes Mai's master is a good man and that some day they will have word of her.

On this bright, sunny morning Star Angel has been asked to do the marketing for the family and so she is standing before one of the stalls, trying to choose the best goose for tonight's dinner. The geese are all lined up, suspended from the metal bar that holds the canvas cover on the top of the stall. Each one is hanging by a hook that goes through the top of its beak. Their feet hang down at the bottom, their toes splayed out. The big, once strong feet of the geese are as different from her own tiny, delicate feet as they can be, Star Angel thinks. Their feathers are plucked and the birds look almost like people, but with very long necks, and they don't appeal to her at all. The fish in the next stall look much better, but she has been instructed to buy a goose and that is what she must buy. The woman in the stall waits expectantly. Star Angel points to the fattest goose and the woman takes it down from its hook.

When it is wrapped in paper and the money has been paid Star Angel buys some leeks and garlic from a vegetable stall and walks slowly through the market on her way out the other side. She sees many things she would like to buy: combs, trinkets for the children, sweets of all kinds, a pretty blouse, a colorful shawl. But she carries no money of her own and only a few extra coins from the household money she has been given, which she cannot use for herself in any event. Her feet have already begun to ache but the walk is a feast for her eyes. Despite the pain, Star Angel loves to be chosen to go to market because it is the only time she can experience all the exotic sights, sounds and smells of the world outside the family's home.

As she reaches the edge of the market area Star Angel sees a man leaning against a tree just at the corner of her vision. A moment of panic comes and goes – she is not sure why, but it is there – and she looks quickly away from his direction. And then a few seconds later she feels a slight rush of air and the goose is whisked from her arms. She is left with only the vegetables. She turns quickly toward the direction of the tree and sees the same man running with her package under his arm and she lets a small scream escape her lips. Not so much as to attract much attention, though, as she has a lifelong habit of keeping herself inconspicuous. Still, a young boy standing nearby, maybe twelve years old, does hear her and looks at Star Angel and then at the man running away and immediately takes off after him.

Star Angel suddenly feels so tired that she lowers herself to the ground and sits with her legs folded under her. She feels that she cannot stand on her painful little stumps of feet any longer.

She watches the man and the boy disappear behind a house and out of sight, and lets a tear roll out of each eye unchecked. She does not know what to do. The boy will catch the man; there is no doubt of that. He is younger and faster and was closing the gap already when they disappeared. But whether he will return with the goose, Star Angel has no way of knowing. And if he doesn't, what will she say to her mother-in-law when she arrives at home without it? Her mother-in-law will blame it on her crossed eye and maybe she will be right. Maybe if her eyes both worked together she would have been able to avoid being surprised by the man. Maybe her mother-in-law will use this as an excuse to throw her out of the house.

And then she sees Lili, who lives just down the road, walking with her little sister, who lives with her in her husband's home. The little girl is only about two or three and is clearly tired and Lili stoops to pick her up and carries her, along with several packages, from the market. Star Angel notes that while Lili's feet are small they are not as small as her own, but still she wonders how she can walk with such a burden.

Lili steps over to where Star Angel is sitting, sets her sister and her packages down on the grass, and sits down with a sigh.

"What's wrong?" she asks.

"I've just bought a goose for dinner," Star Angel says, "and a man grabbed it away from me. I will be beaten or thrown out of the house because of it, I know it." And her two little tears turn into a torrent of noisy sobs as the full impact of what has happened finally hits her and all restraint is abandoned.

"Now, now," says Lili, "surely that young boy will catch the man. I saw them running and I know he will get the goose back for you. All will be well."

Star Angel simply cannot catch her breath. This is the worst thing that has ever happened to her, she thinks. Her fear of being thrown out in the street is so strong. She continues to sob and even the little girl, whose name she does not know, reaches out to touch her arm, as young as she is, knowing that comfort is needed. That quiets Star Angel a bit and she asks the girl her name.

"Coral," she says. "My father called me Sad Coral but Lili says I am not sad and should not say that word. So I am just Coral now. But you are sad. Is your name Sad?"

Star Angel stops her crying at that and looks at the little girl, who has the shiniest black hair and biggest brown eyes she has ever seen, and whose pink dress is well ironed and clean. "No," she says. "I'm not really sad, just now for a few minutes, and that's not my name. I'm Star Angel."

Coral looks up at her big sister. "Lili," she says, "she's not really sad. It's okay."

Lili laughs at that and then Star Angel laughs too. Coral looks back and forth between the two women and then she laughs. And just then the young boy appears, the goose under his arm, and bends down to present it to Star Angel.

"Oh, my. You brought it back. Thank you. Thank you. Here take these." And she pushes two copper coins – the extra bit of money she had – at the boy and he takes them, blushing. He stuffs the coins in his pocket and they all notice a long scar on the top of his left hand, running from his knuckles halfway up his arm toward his elbow.

"I'd be happy to carry the goose home for you," the boy says to Star Angel. "You do look tired."

"Oh, no," she answers. "That will never do. They won't like the looks of it. My talking to a stranger. Even with good reason, it's not allowed. And I can't afford to do anything wrong. I'm not well-liked in the house." At once she feels ashamed. To tell tales of the family to a stranger is very bad. And Lili has witnessed it. But in some way she trusts Lili and doesn't think she would report her. But what she said wasn't strictly true since only one person doesn't like her – her mother-in-law – so she is ashamed of having said an untruth as well.

But she looks hard at the boy, who pulls his scarred arm behind his back, shamed by her stare. "What happened to your arm?" she asks, possibly the boldest question she has ever asked a stranger in her life.

"Just a fight," he mumbles. "It's nothing."

"Did no one try to clean it?" Star Angel asks. "It looks inflamed."

"It's nothing. I have no one to clean it. I've left my family and when I'm old enough I'm going to join the army. Soon. A year maybe. As soon as they will take me. Then I'll have a place to live."

Star Angel does not dare ask him why he left his family. She feels she has already spoken out of turn. But she thinks she can ask his name and does so. He glows at the question, as though it is the first time anyone has been interested enough to care what his name is. He relaxes a bit and lets his arm fall naturally to his side.

"Tiger," he says. "My family called me Tiger Boy, but that is a silly name, a child's name, and I am not a child anymore. So my name is Tiger. When I am an officer in the army that will be a good name for me because I will fight ferociously. All enemies will fall before me."

Star Angel and Lili both laugh at this but they soon see that the boy is quite serious and so they stop laughing and pat him on the back and wish him luck. Coral reaches out and touches his scarred arm, much the same way she touched Star Angel's earlier.

"Don't do that," Lili says to her little sister.

"I just want to know what it feels like," Coral says.

"It's all right," Tiger says. "I don't mind if she touches my scar." He bends down so his face is level with Coral's and looks her straight in the eyes. "It feels a little bumpy," he says. "Go ahead and put your fingers on it and you'll see."

Coral touches the scar again and then pulls her hand back. She doesn't say anything, but she looks into his eyes almost as though intending to memorize his face.

Then Tiger waves cheerfully with his scarred arm as he turns to leave, quickly shoves the hand into his pocket and breaks into a run.

Star Angel puts the goose under her arm, says goodbye to Lili and Coral, and trudges on home with her packages. Relief at having recovered the goose is mixed with exhaustion and worry over the time the whole affair has taken. No doubt it will be remarked upon that she took a long time to buy one goose and some vegetables. But she knows there is no help for that now and is just relieved that she doesn't have to return without the goose.

Inside the house all seems quiet. She leaves the goose and the vegetables in the kitchen and joins the other girls and women in the ladies' parlor. They are all busy with their sewing, the young ones practicing the secret Nu Shu code, each hand being guided by that of an older girl, the women embroidering the code into a tablecloth, each one working at a different section of the beautiful linen cloth. The room is full of whispers and giggles as the closest friends of the girls – their sworn sisters – are here today, too, so all can learn their lessons together. The young girls are giddy with the new language of the thread. Star Angel takes her place at the circle of women working on the tablecloth. She wishes she could have learned this Nu Shu when she was little so it would not be so difficult now. She wishes her eye were not crossed so she would not get a headache when she concentrates on the stitches. She wishes her trip to the market had not been so eventful so she would not now be so exhausted.

But she does not wish anything else to be different. She would not be so tired if she had bigger feet, but she does not wish for bigger feet. She knows her tiny feet are her lifeline. They are what guarantees her place in the family. She sighs and stares at her last Nu Shu symbol and tries to remember what she wanted to say.

What is the story she was trying to tell? And what, she wonders for just a moment, is her old friend Mai sewing right at this moment in her own home? Star Angel holds the needle and makes herself look as busy as she is able. In her heart she is saying a prayer for her womb to fill with a baby boy so she will have two safety nets instead of just one. And all about her the women hum with contentment and gossip and pleasure in their task.

THE MOST BEAUTIFUL GIRL IN THE VILLAGE

"It is better to have a dog than a daughter.
A dog guards the house; a daughter leaves."
—Old Chinese Proverb

Mai was the most beautiful girl in the village, declared so by common consent almost on the day she was born. The birth of a girl was nothing to be celebrated in the little villages of Hunan Province. A girl was considered a liability since she had to be clothed and fed and trained to be a wife. Then she was married out to a husband and his family and that was the end of it. In addition, a dowry had to be provided, and this could be a real hardship if her people were poor.

But a beautiful girl could be an asset, especially if her feet were broken and bound properly, each one shaped into a tiny lotus flower no more than three to five inches long. Then it might be possible to marry her into a very rich and respectable family. And that might bring status and good connections to her birth family.

Besides being beautiful, Mai was a good girl. Even with all the oohing and aahing about her smooth, white skin, her deep brown eyes, her lustrous hair and her heart-shaped lips, she remained sweet tempered and obedient. By the time she was two she could bring tea to her father and older brothers without spilling a drop, and could help her mother with some of the cleaning. By the age of three she was learning to sew and by four she was already mastering some of the symbols of the Nu Shu women's secret writing script and embroidering them into linens. Could there be a sweeter picture than beautiful little Mai sitting quietly at the age of six and embroidering Nu Shu into the strips of cloth that would soon be used to bind her feet?

When her mother began the process of foot binding Mai did not complain. She fought back her tears so her mother would not have an unpleasant reminder of the pain she was causing her darling child. And when it was time to learn to walk on her broken feet, to learn to balance and to develop that charming sway of the hips that men love so much, she did not scream in pain and throw herself down on the floor and refuse to move as so many other little girls did. No, she bit her lower lip till it bled so she would not feel the pain in her feet, and she walked. She lowered her eyelids to keep the tears inside and she walked. She clenched her little fists until the palms of her hands had red welts from her finger nails digging into them, and she stumbled and stumbled, but she walked.

And Mai was a help to her friends too as they went through the same process of having their feet broken so they would be beautiful to men. Sometimes her best friend and sworn sister, Star Angel, would visit and they would learn the Nu Shu together from Mai's cousin. Star Angel could not really learn it properly because one of her eyes turned in and she did not see the symbols clearly. Mai would throw her arms around Star Angel's neck and comfort her. She would tell Star Angel that her feet were the tiniest and prettiest of anyone's and that she didn't need to worry about learning Nu Shu, that she would be totally happy without it. She would make Star Angel smile and Star Angel loved Mai for that.

By the time Mai was eight she was as perfect as she could be. Already the families of young village boys were calling with gifts and trying to arrange a betrothal for their sons. But though Mai's family was poor that did not mean they were not smart. They knew they had a precious jewel and they were not going to give it away to just anyone who brought a gift. In fact, the collecting of gifts turned into quite a profitable business for Mai's parents and they continued it for many years. Over time her reputation as a lovely, cultured and dutiful young woman spread far beyond the village and gifts came from every direction and from great distances.

Mai's father and mother were just at the point, when Mai was seventeen, of thinking that it was time to accept an offer. Soon Mai would begin to be too old, her beauty would begin to decline, she would become worthless. Her dearest friend, Star Angel, had already been given as a concubine to one of the better families. Not as good as a marriage, perhaps, but secure enough. Mai had her own ideas on this subject but she did not share them with her father, who would make the final decision about her life. She knew her input was not required or desired. Her father would never even discuss the subject with her. But the truth was, Mai was in love with the young man who lived down the road and sold fruit from his family's orchard at the market on Wednesday mornings.

Every week when Mai did the marketing for her mother she would linger as long as possible at Chang's stall. She loved to talk to him about everything in her life and he enjoyed her visits, which helped the time pass for him. He told her that he did not really like selling fruit in the market and she told him that she did not like many of her chores at home. Neither ever mentioned their growing attraction to each other because they knew it didn't make any difference. Both would have marriages arranged for them by their fathers. And neither would have any say in the choice, which would be made strictly on the basis of economics. Since Mai was the most beautiful girl in the village, and sought after by all the wealthy families, Chang's family would never even try to get her, even if they knew their son loved her. And if they were so foolish as to try they would be laughed at because many rich suitors had already been rejected as Mai's family waited for the best opportunity. Nobody likes to be laughed at.

So, not knowing or caring what Mai might want, her parents began to discuss which of the offers still available they would take. Which young man's family would bring the most in terms of status, even money – since Mai was such a prize – to have this beauty in their household?

Just as Mai's parents were narrowing the choices and getting ready to accept an offer, a most amazing thing happened. Word came to them that the highest official in the province of Hunan had heard of Mai's beauty and wanted her for a concubine. This was the ultimate in good luck for the family, something they had never dared to hope for. To be connected to the authorities in this way would bring not only status but protection. Mai's mother and father looked at each other smugly. It had been well worth waiting until Mai was seventeen to find the perfect match for her, even if it turned out she would be a concubine and not a wife. They had enriched their coffers with many splendid gifts from suitors and now could turn Mai over to a household that could almost be considered royalty. No one could cry foul since this was an obvious choice and no other family could compete. There was rejoicing everywhere as this match would bring glory to the whole village. Only Mai was silent. Not complaining, just silent. Fierce Shadow, the highest official in Hunan Province, who had set his eye on seventeen year old Mai, the prettiest girl in the village, and was now to have her for his concubine, was seventy-eight years old.

On the day that Mai was to be brought to the man to become his concubine, her mother helped her dress in her finest clothes. All she owned – her clothes, her combs, her makeup, her tiny shoes, and the cloths she needed to wrap her feet each night to keep their beautiful size and shape – were packed in her trunk. Her mother could sense that Mai was sad and urged her to take heart.

"Even though you are not marrying," she told her, "you will be a concubine in the richest, most powerful household in the entire province. That is truly better. You will live in splendor, among important people. You will never want for anything. And maybe you will even be able to secure important positions for your brothers in the household or in the government. You are a very lucky girl."

Mai did not feel lucky. She silently cursed her great beauty. Without it she might have married Chang, or even one of the other attractive young men of the village. She might now be in the grass behind her house exchanging sweet kisses with Chang and talking of their future. But she knew what her mother said was true and she would never be anything but the obedient child she had been raised to be. So Mai said nothing of her true feelings, of the young man she loved, and instead prepared to move to her new home and say goodbye to her family, probably forever. Of the loss of Chang or of her family, she was not sure which stung her heart more.

At the appointed hour, two of the high official's servants arrived in a carriage. A grand carriage, indeed. It was painted white and the windows were covered with heavy red brocade curtains so no one could look in. It seemed all the town rushed out of their homes to watch as Mai was helped into the carriage and carried away. They had never seen anything like this before. They were all terribly proud to know a girl so beautiful that the richest man in the province had chosen her to be his concubine. The other girls, including two of her closest friends who were still unmarried, could barely contain their jealousy.

But once the carriage began to move, and Mai was safely behind the curtained windows, she allowed herself to cry. To sob heavily, in fact, for more than an hour, until she finally fell asleep. When she arrived at her grand new home she was awakened rudely by the driver and rushed from the carriage, her face all blotchy and her makeup smeared from her tears. Her hair was askew from the way her head had been pressed against the side of the carriage during her short nap. It is safe to say that in her entire life, up to that moment, the beautiful Mai had never looked so disheveled.

She was met inside the gates by a tall, severe woman who hustled her into a large room and allowed her a few minutes to go to the bathroom, then led her down a long, dark corridor toward what Mai hoped was her bedroom. But it was not. It was the office of Fierce Shadow, the man who was to be like a husband to her but not a real husband because he already had a wife. And fourteen concubines. And twenty-two sons and fifteen daughters, many of them older than Mai.

Mai looked at Fierce Shadow and her heart sank. He was old, and she expected that. But he was ugly too, the kind of ugly that would have been horrible even when he was young. It came from meanness, and Mai, though she was young and inexperienced and had been treated with deference all of her beautiful life, was able to recognize the shallowness and meanness of spirit etched into the deep lines of the man's face. It was a face that did not smile often; anger was written all over it. Her heart sank, even as she fell to her knees in the bow her mother had taught her to make. And she expected to see his face melt at her beauty – that was what she was accustomed to – but it did not. Instead, he roared up from his chair and yelled to the woman standing beside Mai, "Take her out of here and clean her up and bring her to me after dinner."

When Mai reached her new living quarters she was shocked in two ways. First, in so fine a house as this she expected a comfortable room, more comfortable certainly than the room she had in her childhood home. But it was not so. This was little more than a cell with a cot and a basin for water. There was a stand for her trunk and two drawers for her clothes. There was a small, square window with no curtain to cover it. The woman handed her a little mirror and she had her second shock. She saw how her makeup had run all over her face and how messy her hair was. And she knew what a terrible impression she must have made on Fierce Shadow. That she vowed to correct, and show him this evening how beautiful she really was. And, she thought, I will earn his love and get a better room than this. He is not sure of me yet, so he has put me here. When he knows the real me he will love me.

After a small dinner of porridge and a hard roll, taken in her sparse room, Mai was brought to the man she would serve that night. She had made herself beautiful again, but he had not taken the same pains with himself. The minute she stepped over the threshold into his room she could smell the alcohol on his breath and as she drew nearer the smell grew stronger, mixed with a smell of body odor she had not noticed in his office a few hours earlier. He called her to him and she obeyed, as the tall woman silently backed out of the room and closed the door. She obeyed him in everything, doing whatever he asked of her and choking back the nausea when the smells of the man or the things she was asked to do for him proved more than she could stomach. But she did not complain and she did not cry.

They stayed in that room together for three days and three nights. Food was brought to them every few hours. Fierce Shadow ate and drank but Mai refused the food and only sipped some tea occasionally to keep up her strength. Fierce Shadow did not care if she ate or not. He did not speak to her when he ate. He slept little but when he did Mai sat silently and closed her eyes but sleep would not come.

At the dawn of what would have been their fourth day together, Fierce Shadow awoke and looked at Mai and said, "Go to your room. You are useless." So Mai got up and hastily put on her clothes and left Fierce Shadow's quarters. She found her way back to her own room and fell on the cot and sobbed until at last she fell asleep.

Mai never saw Fierce Shadow again and she was never moved to larger quarters. She passed her time in her little room embroidering Nu Shu into linens the family gave her. She was given the smallest amount of food that could sustain her and in the winter there was so little heat provided that she had to use her

Nu Shu linens as extra covers when she slept on her cot. She had not become pregnant during her three days with the old man so she had no child, neither boy nor girl, to raise or to comfort her. And so, of course, she had no status in the family either. She mingled very seldom with the other concubines. But some of their children were kind to her and visited her in her room, taking a meal with her sometimes and talking with her of life in the rest of the house and in the gardens where Mai, so placid and timid, never dared to venture.

When Mai was twenty-five years old, Fierce Shadow died. Although she was only his concubine, his death made Mai a widow, as it did all the concubines. Remarriage for widows was frowned upon; it made a woman almost as much of an outcast as being a widow did. Society had no place for such creatures. And Mai would not have wanted to marry anyway. She considered herself lucky to be able to continue to live in the household of Fierce Shadow, which was now ruled by his sons. She could not secure any prominent positions for her brothers, as her parents had hoped would happen. But she did not have to return to her parents or live in the streets, either of which would have been a disgrace.

Sometimes she thought of Chang and wondered which girl his father had chosen for him to marry and whether they had children. And whether he ever thought of her. Sometimes she thought of her old friend Star Angel, who had also become a concubine, and wondered if she had been any luckier in the master she served and how many children she had. She imagined that maybe Star Angel had given birth to many boys and been exalted to a high position in her family. She pictured her sitting and sewing with the other concubines, Star Angel the one they all looked up to because she had given birth to so many boys.

Many years later, Mai wrote in Nu Shu on a fan she made as a gift for one of Fierce Shadow's daughters, "I think I died at twenty-five when my master died."

LETTER TO MY DAUGHTER

*"Some men know how to plant the seeds
but they do not know how to tend the garden."*
—Anonymous Nu Shu

To my dear daughter, my child now grown, who lives in Lonely River,

I embroider these words on a fan and send them to you as a gift. I will have someone bring this fan to you as I cannot carry it myself on my bound feet. I want you to know that I love you and I know how hard it is to suffer as a young bride at the hands of a cruel man. If my own husband, your father, were still alive I would not be able to tell him that I was writing the Nu Shu script or sending you this fan.

Now that I am old I live with my son, your brother. When you are a girl at home you obey your father. When you're married you obey your husband. And when your husband dies you obey your son. That is why a woman must give birth to a son, at least one. If not, she will have no place in her husband's family and they will mistreat her if they wish to. Then, when her husband dies, she will have no one to take care of her. But all this you know and have known since you were a little girl as you can see what is all around you.

Many women live on the street because they have no husbands and no living sons and they are not allowed to marry again. Some women do remarry anyway but they are scorned by all, even their own children because they have brought disgrace on their entire family. You must be certain never to do anything that will disgrace your husband's family or you will surely suffer greatly for it.

Last year, when my husband died, I was left living with my son and his wife. I didn't like that arrangement from the first, because I don't like my son, your brother, at all. He has grown up to be a tyrant just like his father. But his wife was a sweet girl and she was about to give birth to their first child and that would give me something to do. At least I would be needed. I tried to be a kind mother-in-law, though that is a very rare type of person, indeed. I'm glad I made the effort, though, because my daughter-in-law did not live very long. She died giving birth to their baby and that made me very sad. Now I have to live with my son, who is meaner than ever. I am very unhappy. But there is no other place for a woman like me.

The baby is a boy and that is good. It means good luck for the family. And he is a good baby. He does not cry too much and he is easy to care for. So that part of my life is a blessing. But we have had a drought here for many years and then we had a flood. Life is hard for women now because when times are bad they always think it's the women's fault. They say the women did something to offend the gods and turn everything bad. So I stay quiet and just take care of my grandson while my son works in the fields. The landlord won't reduce the farmers' burden, even in these hard times. He won't charge less rent or require fewer crops in payment for our small cottage.

I am glad my grandson is still a baby because young men in this village are joining the army and going to fight. There is no other way for them to earn a living so they go, even if they don't want to and their mothers don't want them to. Sometimes the mothers never hear from them again. Sometimes someone brings their bodies back. And sometimes they come back alive, but not too often. Five young men from our village left this morning. I cried for them and their mothers. One very nice young boy, called Tiger Boy, has left his family already. He is too young to go into the army yet, but he is going to try and I won't be surprised if they take him anyway. They are so desperate for new blood. I know that sounds harsh, but he is such an innocent child and I fear he is lost already.

Last week all the men in the village went to see a pretty tea girl in another village several miles away. My son went with them. He was very excited about the trip and said the girl is the most beautiful tea girl who has ever been in our county. Now all the wives have three days to sit and sew together. Even though I am a grandmother, they let me join them. We took a large tablecloth and each embroidered a corner. Then we turned the tablecloth and read each other's writing. This brings peace and friendship into our lives. We are so happy when the men leave. I am the luckiest because all the young girls have mothers-in-law who tell them what to do. And they have to hide their Nu Shu from them. But I have only my son and when he leaves I can do anything I want.

There is a family in our village that had four sons and no daughters. I think you will remember them from when you were growing up. They are the Li family. They were the luckiest family I ever knew, even looking back to when I was a young girl. Because the four sons were so good and worked together, the family had enough money to buy some land and so the work they did on this land was all for the benefit of their entire family. They grew many crops and rented out a small portion of the land to another family who worked for them. They were very prosperous and in our poor village they were easily the wealthiest people.

All the boys made excellent marriages when they reached the proper age. Who wouldn't want their daughters to marry into this lucky family? From what I know of the mother, Li Iris, she was a fair and reasonable mother-in-law. They built two additions to their little house so the whole family could live together. And each of the wives had at least one son, although some had daughters as well. But even the daughters were not a burden because there was enough money to make good dowries for all of them. So everything was very good for the family for many years. Much of this you may remember.

But listen to what happened to them. A few months ago the

father died. Then all the sons and their wives began to argue about the land. They couldn't decide how to share the work now that the father was gone. They couldn't agree to let one of them be the boss of the operation. So they decided to split up the land and divide the house into separate buildings. They are spending money on breaking apart their house, money that could have been spent on food and clothes. They argue all the time, even when others are near enough to hear them.

I met one of the daughters-in-law at the market the other day and she said all the daughters-in-law were willing to continue to share as they used to. But the sons would not ask for their opinions and would not listen if their wives tried to talk to them about the problem. Women do not know anything about business, they say when one of the wives tries to speak. So they are tearing apart their land and their house and even their family because the men cannot agree on anything and will not accept advice from the women. But when their lives become poor because of the men's bad decisions they will say it is the women's fault, just as they always do when something bad happens. They will say the women have angered the gods.

My dear daughter, I hope you love me and do not blame me for the match your father and I made for you. I was diligent in your foot binding and I think we made the best match for you we could, even with our meager funds for your dowry. But there is never any way to tell if a new husband will be kind or if his mother will be fair to her new daughter-in-law. Not that that would have been a consideration for your father in any event.

I am happy for you that you have a son, but you also have a daughter and I hold my breath for her safety. I beg you to bind her feet properly for her entire future depends upon it. If her feet are not small enough, if they do not have the perfect lotus shape, she will not fetch a husband with money. Your heart will break with every bone that breaks in her tiny feet, but you must do it. And take care that the bandages are always kept clean so infection does not set in. If you are unable to marry her off in a good match, and it is because her feet are not perfect, you will be blamed for this.

But I beg you, also, to teach your daughter the Nu Shu. This is just as important as binding her feet. It will help her to be part of a community that will support her. If her marriage is difficult, as is likely to be the case, sewing Nu Shu will give her a way to express her sadness, even if there is never anyone to read her words. This I did for you and this you must also do for your most precious daughter.

I am almost forty years old now and I have seen a lot. I know only two villages, the one I was born in and the one I was married out to, so I can't say much of the larger world. But I know how people are: how women can be kind to their Nu Shu sisters and carry them through the most awful losses. I appreciate the news you have sent me on occasion of Mai and Star Angel, Lili and Coral, and some of the other women who live in your village or are friends of your friends. These stories have helped me to learn more of life than I might otherwise ever know.

Life is mostly about loss in the end. But I know that men do not share that feeling of kindness for women. At least not the men I have encountered. So you must look out for yourself. Put by a little money from the household cash whenever you can. You may need that to supplement your daughter's dowry when the time comes. And if this should happen, devise a way that your husband will not know what you have done or he will watch you more carefully afterward and be suspicious all the time. He will not appreciate what you have accomplished as it was done behind his back.

Be kind to your mother-in-law as much as you can. Even if she does not deserve it. You may need her to be on your side at some time. Mothers-in-law have been brides too, and except for the meanest among them, they do remember what it was like. And most remember the Nu Shu, too, and how they used it sometimes just to keep themselves from going into madness in hard times. Maybe your mother-in-law will help you hide your Nu Shu from your husband if that becomes necessary. I would have done that in a heartbeat for my daughter-in-law if she had lived.

I don't know if Lonely River is a good place to live but I hope it is. I hope the women help each other when they can, and sit together in the afternoon or evening and sew Nu Shu. Hold your women friends dear to your heart as they are the ones who will always be there for you. That will make your life more bearable. But even if the women in your village are not a comfort, never forget your Nu Shu and sew it yourself every evening. That way you will not forget your memories, and will have your work for a comfort in your old age.

I hope this fan arrives safely and brings news from a mother you love and think of often. Know that I think of you and love you and hope your life is not too hard. If someday we can meet again in this life it will make me very happy. Be strong for your children's sakes and do not let your husband or his family see you cry. Let the Nu Shu I taught you, and the memory of our hours together while you were learning it, be a comfort for you when times are difficult.

This fan is a gift from your loving mother.

PART THREE — 1940

PART THREE - 1940—

DEATHS IN THE FAMILY

*"You push aside a dark cloud and
then you will see the blue sky;
women wait for the hard luck to be over
so they can have a better life."*
—Anonymous Nu Shu

Down the road from the house where Lili lived with her sons and her husband and his family and her sister Coral, an elderly woman named Pearl lived alone. Lili visited her often, mostly to keep her company as she had the time now that her two sons were married and her daughters-in-law did much of the household work. And Pearl appreciated the visits because she had no one else to talk to and she needed to tell someone her unhappy history. Lili always listened politely and commiserated with Pearl, a plain woman with sad eyes, on her bad luck in life. Sometimes Coral would accompany her sister on these visits when she could spare the time from her household tasks.

It was during one of these afternoon visits that Pearl first told her history to Lili over cups of steaming tea.

"I am part of an unfortunate family," Pearl began. "It is hard enough to be born a girl but if there are some boys in the family at least you know your mother will be all right. But in my family there were no boys. My mother had only two girls. She might yet have had a boy, or many boys, but my father died when I was only seven. And then my sister, still just a baby, died. So we were just my mother and me. A widow and a daughter. No father to protect us. No son or brother to go to work. My mother was sad because of the losses in her life. And I was sad because of our loneliness."

"How did you manage?" Lili asked.

"We both had to work to stay alive," Pearl said. "We had no one else to depend on."

"What work did you do?"

"I worked in the rice fields and earned a spoon of rice for every cup of rice I husked for others. That is very exact. I always knew how close I was getting to a meal as the day passed by. I seemed to watch my dinner grow larger as I worked, and gauged my growing hunger against my strength to work. But I was young and strong then and husked enough for myself and enough left over to supplement my mother's harvest as well. So we both had the rice we needed to sustain us."

Pearl leaned back in her chair and sighed. Lili did not like to press her for details, but Pearl seemed to want to talk. So she asked, "Didn't anyone ever help you?"

"People do not like to help a widow or a girl without a father. They think our bad luck will come to them, too, if they get too close. Sometimes we cut firewood on the mountain and fixed the canals in the fields. People disliked it if we asked them to help us even with the very heavy work. I was always sad to see my small, worn mother doing the same hard work as I. But no one worked with us. We had no one to help us."

The women sipped their tea and Lili turned the conversation to more pleasant topics.

Some afternoons when Lili and Coral both came to visit, the three would work together in Pearl's garden. Pearl lived on a very tiny budget, provided by two cousins who helped support her, and needed the vegetables from her garden to supplement her diet.

On one such afternoon, Pearl took up her story again and Lili and Coral listened.

"When I was seventeen my mother handed me over to the Lu family," she began. "She married me out. My dowry was less than the dowries of other girls but the Lu family was nice and treated me kindly. My husband had two older sisters who hadn't married out yet and two younger brothers and we all worked together and got along together as friends would. When I was twenty-two I bore a son and was happy. Everyone was happy. When I was twenty-four I gave birth to a daughter and no one treated me badly because of it. I was content with my life, which was better than I could have ever hoped."

Pearl's face clouded over and she swallowed hard. Lili thought this might be the end of the story but she knew Pearl had never before mentioned having children or grandchildren so she began to get a tight feeling in her stomach, almost afraid to hear what might be coming next.

Pearl seemed to be trying to pull herself together, as if she were determined to tell the whole story no matter how much pain the telling caused.

"How could I have known?" she asked. "How could anyone have known that when I was twenty-seven my children would suddenly have sores? After ten days they had fever and rashes, and the rashes would not clear. I held them and rocked them. I sang over them and cried over them. I tried every remedy that my mother-in-law and her friends suggested. I would have done anything to make them well again. My husband's hair turned gray with worry. And then my children died. Both of them. Within two hours of each other."

Coral had her hands over her heart and was crying. Lili just looked at Pearl with a mixture of shock and pity. She could not even reach out to her at first, but finally she got out of her chair and put her arms around the older woman.

"Oh, Pearl," she said, "that must have been so hard to bear."

"I felt as though I had lost my soul," Pearl said. "I became an empty shell. My husband's family was kind to me, kinder than they should have been because my bad luck could easily have rubbed off on them. I was grateful for their kindness, but nothing could make me happy again."

Then Pearl said that she left her husband, and Lili and Coral were both surprised.

"When my children died it was as if I had died too. I wanted to go back to my mother, who was just as alone as I was. I understood how alone she felt because she too had had a child die. My husband was a good man and he said I could go back to my mother for a visit. His brother's son came to take me home to distract me from my sadness. But I was sad at home too when I thought of all the bad luck my family and I had.

"Still, even amid the deaths and bad luck, we had some goodness come to us. My mother was now raising two nephews because her husband's brother had died and then his wife died and left these two boys. Despite the misery of two more deaths, it was good for my mother because now she had two boys to take care of her in her old age. I decided to stay with my mother to help her with the boys. I knew that the boys would take care of me too when I followed my mother into old age."

Pearl looked tired now and Lili put out her hand to tell her to rest.

Pearl said, "My mouth is dry and my mind is tired, but first I want to tell you why I never went back to my husband and his family." Lili sat back again.

"Although they never treated me badly there were so many sad memories from my children dying that I could not go back there. And my husband had a concubine now who had already given him a son and might give him more. So he did not need me. He was a good man who would have taken me back but I might never have had sons there to protect me so I didn't want to go."

Just as Lili was thinking she and Coral must go and let Pearl rest, there was a knock at the door. The women looked at each other in surprise as neither could imagine who the unexpected visitor could be. Pearl arose from her chair with an air of weariness and straightened her apron. She walked to the door and opened it to find a man standing there. A man she didn't know, who might have been about her age, late forties or so. He carried a travel bag – not a very big one – and had kind eyes, which Pearl trusted at once. He looked past the door into the house and then asked the women if he could trouble them for a drink of water, as he had traveled far on foot and still had a way to go. He'd heard their voices from outside, he said, and thought they sounded friendly.

Pearl didn't hesitate for a moment. She invited him to step inside the door and hurried to get a cup of cool water for him. He wore a gray cap, which he removed, and bowed deeply as he took the water from her hands. As he sipped from the cup, slowly and with obvious pleasure, a pang of guilt struck deep in Pearl's heart. She knew she was a woman of bad luck and that bad luck can rub off on anyone who comes too near. She worried that the man, not knowing her, did not know the chance he was taking by standing inside her door and drinking her water. She looked at Lili and Coral with alarm.

Before any of the women could say anything, the man said, "Thank you, madam, for your generosity. I would like to just rest a while here and then treat you to a small meal at the tea shop down the road. Your husband, too, is most welcome to join us. Or a son, perhaps?"

"I cannot accept your most gracious offer since I have neither husband nor son to accompany me," Pearl said. This was not the answer she wished to give, but the one she knew she must give as it would not do for her to be seen with a stranger in the tea shop. She felt a mixture of disappointment and relief when she said the words. She would have enjoyed a meal in the tea shop and conversation with someone new, but she was happy she did not have to wrestle with the decision. It was not allowed and the price she would pay for such an indiscretion would far outweigh any pleasure of the outing. As a woman living alone she had to be careful every moment to be sure she behaved correctly or the wrath of the town would be upon her at once. Even the friendship of her respected friend, Lili, would not be enough to protect her.

The gentleman bowed again, quite deeply this time. He understood, and did not press the point. "May I just sit outside on your step then and finish this water? I am only a traveler looking for a few moments of rest."

Pearl nodded and the man went outside and she closed the door softly. Lili much admired her friend's composure and Coral had learned a lesson in etiquette and the moral standards of Lonely River. Lili thought they would leave now, but Pearl sat down again and seemed to want to continue talking.

"I just want to tell you the rest of how I came to be here in this house alone," she said. "After my mother reached her old age and died her nephews, my cousins, took care of me out of honor toward my mother who had raised them, and because they had grown into kind men. Both married and had sons and daughters and I loved them all. I taught the daughters our beloved Nu Shu script so they could record their memories and tell their stories to their friends and children and to each other. When they married out they sent me many fans and handkerchiefs that told of their lives in beautiful Nu Shu embroidery. I am proud that even though my own daughter died I was able to pass on the Nu Shu. And I am happy that in my old age I receive many gifts of Nu Shu that provide pleasant hours of reading and beautiful decorations for my simple home, the same cottage I was born in."

Lili sighed deeply, knowing the story was, at last, finished. Coral looked at Pearl with a mixture of admiration and fear in her face. She was wondering what her life would be like when she was as old as Pearl. Only in the last couple of years had she become aware that she would likely never marry because Lili had not bound her feet. What man would ever want her? And without a husband, how would she have children to take care of her? Lili had told her many times that it is not necessary to bind one's feet anymore and that plenty of men will want to marry her, but Coral was not so sure. She didn't know any girls her age whose feet were not bound. And whenever she studied Nu Shu with her friends, her sworn sisters, she was sure they were staring at her feet, maybe even laughing when she looked the other way.

Lili had told Coral that when it was time to bind her feet she had been hearing that foot binding was now outlawed. She said she asked many people about it and, though some had also heard the same thing, no one was actually thinking of not binding their daughters' feet. But Coral was not Lili's daughter and the household had no stake in her future except that they would like to see her married at some time. But they felt that if Lili didn't mind Coral staying on as a servant girl they didn't either and they didn't interfere with Lili's decision.

Lili said Coral should not pay any attention to that kind of talk – she would not live out her days as a servant girl. Lili told Coral that she would be independent, have a job – maybe be a nurse or work in an office somewhere – and she would be fine even if she didn't marry. But Coral was not so sure about any of this and she tucked her big feet under her chair so Pearl and Lili would not notice them.

At last Lili and Coral rose to leave, taking their tea cups to the kitchen sink on their way out the door.

"Come back soon for another visit," Pearl called out as the two stepped gingerly around the gentleman traveler, who was still sitting on the steps of the tiny porch. Lili and Coral waved and started on down the path.

As soon as they were out of sight Pearl went down the steps and began pulling weeds from her garden. The gentleman traveler did not move and after a while she went inside, washed her hands and returned with a table cloth she was embroidering as a gift for one of her nieces. It had a design that went round and round the edge of the cloth three times. It was a pattern made from Nu Shu symbols and told something of her life. Pearl looked slyly at the man and then began to sew the symbols that would tell of his visit.

After a while the man asked to see the cloth and said he admired the beauty of the work. Pearl did not tell him the characters she was sewing told a story, but he wanted to see how she formed them and she let him look more closely as she sewed. He watched for some time – until he noticed the sun beginning to lower in the western sky.

"This has been a most pleasant afternoon and a sweet rest from my travels," he said as he rose from the step with amazing ease and bowed deeply. "I believe I will stop the night at the inn and perhaps say goodbye to you in the morning as I resume my journey. I hope you know that it is possible to make a new friend, even later in life, and that you might consider me such a friend so we can speak again when I pass this way on my return."

He touched Pearl's hand lightly, which was a surprise to her and a good feeling, too. No man had touched her hand for many years. But, also, she felt a pang of guilt because she had not warned him of her bad luck. She thought that maybe her bad luck had lost its power after all those years and that if he really returns she could believe that was true. Still, she thought, maybe I am wicked to allow such a nice man to take that risk. Pearl sighed. She didn't know what to think, but she allowed the desires of her heart to rule her head and nodded and said she hoped to see him again. And with that he left.

Pearl stayed outside and picked up her sewing again as she watched the man disappear down the path. Around the border of her tablecloth it said in the Nu Shu symbols she had learned as a child, "I have both tears and joy in my life. I thank my mother for marrying me out and taking me back and teaching me Nu Shu so I never forget."

And to that she added, "I thank the great world for giving me a wonderful afternoon and a possibility of more."

THE GOOD LUCK GIRL

"Everybody has their turn; someday it will be the women's turn."
—Anonymous Nu Shu

John Chung slammed both his hands down on the table and glared at the four men sitting with him. They were old friends, good friends, who had grown up together and attended school with him. All were in their late twenties, successful land owners and businessmen with wives and families and, in some cases, concubines.

But John was a little different from the others, and growing more so by the day. For one thing, he had taken a foreign first name, and had rearranged his names so his family name was second, in the foreign way. This, he said, was a help when doing business with foreigners as they didn't understand the Chinese way of putting the family name first and got confused and then embarrassed when they addressed him incorrectly. None of the other men did business with foreigners so they could not understand the importance of making this change.

"Why shouldn't I take my wife with me on a business trip?" John asked, glaring at the men.

"Because," said Fortune's Son, John's best friend, "there are women everywhere. What do you need a wife for?"

John sighed and shook his head. He knew by now that he would never make his friends understand. In some strange way he had simply left them behind. Their wives were nothing more than sex objects to them, bearers of their children, which had better be boys, people they rarely if ever had a conversation with. But John's wife was like a partner to him. She was smart and had good ideas about his exporting business. And she was beautiful and strong. Even with her bound feet she could keep up pretty well with the wives of the foreign businessmen they met. And those wives fussed over his Jasmine, examined her tiny shoes and the combs in her hair and her clothes. She was a real asset to him on business trips, but his friends had no idea about the sort of world John traveled in.

When he married Jasmine, John knew that she was what was called a good luck girl. Everyone in her village and all the surrounding villages, including his, knew that she was born under lucky stars and planets and that a fortune teller had announced to her family that she was going to bring good luck to them and to the family that she married into. She was pretty, too, with big brown eyes and smooth, white skin. By the time she was four years old, Jasmine was already wanted for marriage by many families. She was thirteen and a half when John married her and he had always been good to her. Not only because he believed she would bring him luck, but because of her beauty and how smart she was. And he loved her. Everyone knew, too, that since John had married Jasmine there had not been a flood or a drought in Lonely River. It would be impossible to ignore the connection.

John never tried to steal or ruin Jasmine's Nu Shu embroidery. He didn't know exactly what it was, but he knew it was important, not only because she treasured it so much, but because other women gave her their embroidery to keep for them because they feared their own husbands would ruin or steal theirs. He knew that Jasmine was proud that she could protect her friends' handiwork and that they all knew she did not fear her husband. In fact he would have felt terrible if she did fear him.

Sometimes Jasmine shared stories with John that she heard about her friends. He never knew exactly how women heard these stories, but there were many things he didn't understand about women. Jasmine told him once that a woman from her birth village, who had grown up by her side, was married and had four daughters before she finally had a son. But the boy was sick and died just a few hours after he was born. When her husband and mother-in-law found out they beat her, before she had even recovered from the birth. The next day, when she had some of her strength back, she hanged herself. The husband remarried, his new wife gave him a son quickly, and the four daughters were thrown out of the house. John was appalled at that story. He could not begin to comprehend such cruelty.

When John was a schoolboy, when he was still Chung Lo and still under the influence of his friends, he watched his two younger sisters, each in her turn, go through the process of having her feet bound. He saw how much pain they were in, how they cried, secretly, when they thought no one was watching. He mentioned the painful scenes he had witnessed to his friends but they only laughed. "It will all be worthwhile for them because they will get good husbands. Girls aren't worth anything without their husbands. Who cares if they cry?" they said.

John asked his mother about it and she told him that he must always respect women, if only because they were so dependent on their husbands. She set a good example too when he married, because she was never cruel to Jasmine as so many other mothers-in-law were to the girls their sons married. Now he saw that being kind to Jasmine was well worthwhile because she had turned out to be such a help to him.

So, despite the laughter of his friends, who didn't understand anything anyway, John and Jasmine set out by coach for Ji'an, traveling slowly and enjoying the sights of the road. They were to meet some businessmen and county officials to close a deal he had been working on for months. His work had already been complicated by the war that was gripping his country and much of the world, and he wanted to close the negotiations at last. When they arrived they were both tired but they had an appointment to meet the men -- six in all -- for dinner, so they went to their hotel room and changed quickly.

When they entered the restaurant, all six men were already seated and there was one empty chair at the table. The highest county official looked at John and said, "We have women coming later. We will not need this one but she can eat in the kitchen if you have promised her dinner."

"This is my wife, Jasmine," John said. "She will eat with us." And he signaled the waiter to bring another chair.

The county official, dressed in a foreign-style business suit, bald, overweight and self-important, turned quite red in the face. The other men either laughed or looked down at the table in embarrassment. What were they to do with this wife when the party women arrived later, the official wondered. Surely the wife could not join them, he knew, but would John Chung leave the group or take his wife back to their hotel room and rejoin the men later? He had no idea; he had never encountered such a situation before.

So the men talked and laughed – John too – and just generally ignored Jasmine. She never spoke a word. She sat there in her exquisite blue dress with the tiny flowers she had sewn on herself and kept her eyes on her dinner plate, pushing her food around with her chopsticks, but barely eating a bite. She wished there were some foreign men in the group because they would have spoken to her, might have even had their wives with them, but there were none this time and Jasmine felt quite out of place.

When the dinner finally ended there was some hushed talk about women and hotel rooms and John took Jasmine's elbow and guided her carefully to the restaurant door as she stepped daintily on her tiny feet.

"No, no," the official was saying as he rushed to John's side before they could get out of the restaurant. He had clearly had an idea, an inspiration of some sort, and was looking at the entire incident in a new way.

"Bring her along. We understand she is not really your wife. And she is quite lovely." He bowed a small courteous bow to Jasmine. "The men are interested. They want her to join the party."

"In fact she is my wife."

"I'm sorry," said the official, "but there is no way we can close our deal except at our party. And we want this woman to attend. Bring her along, please."

Despite the use of the word please, it was an order, not a request, and John knew it. Jasmine's face reddened, whether with anger or embarrassment one couldn't say for sure. She touched John's arm and he could feel the panic in her fingers. She trusted him, but this was business. And business comes first for men, she knew, even a man as good as her husband.

"I will meet you and the rest of the gentlemen back at the hotel in one hour," John said and bowed deeply. He guided Jasmine through the door and they disappeared into the dark night.

When they were in their hotel room John instructed Jasmine to prepare for bed and not wait for him. "I'll be back when I can," he said. "The county has already approved my contract, the rest of them will go along with the details, and I'll be back before the party starts. I will make apologies for you; I'll say you're ill. They won't even remember once the other women arrive. I must hurry to get it all done while they are still sober enough to sign the contracts."

When John arrived at the party he was clapped on the back and congratulated for having brought such a beautiful woman with him. As he expected, they did not really mind that she was not joining the party as they had several women there. After he had their signatures on his contracts he told them again that Jasmine was truly his wife. They laughed again. "It would have cost less to get a woman here than to bring your wife and feed her for so many days on the road," the fat county official said. John laughed with them and patted his pocket where the signed contracts lay folded safely and neatly.

In the hotel room Jasmine sat in their bed and looked around. She hadn't had much of a chance to examine the room when they rushed in earlier to change their clothes for dinner. It was the most elegant room she'd ever seen. There were silk curtains on the windows and a silk cover on the bed. They had their own bathroom, not shared with other rooms. It was the most spacious and comfortable arrangement and she wished she could always live in a place like this.

Jasmine knew her husband preferred her to strange women and she felt treasured because of it. She had read enough of her sworn sisters' Nu Shu embroidery to know that this is not what most husbands think. "It is because I am a good luck girl that he cares for me so much," she thought.

She took out a small piece of Nu Shu that she had brought with her to work on and she sewed these words: "My husband is a learned man. Once he went to the capital of Hunan Province to take the court writing test, which he passed with honor. This means he could leave the village permanently for an important job with the government if he wants to. His mother and the rest of the family all worry that he may do this because they don't want him to leave. But I don't worry because I know that if he goes he will take me with him, even against everybody's objections. And he will take our sons, too, because I could not bear to be apart from them for too long. He would never do anything to make me unhappy because I am a good luck girl."

When John returned he saw that Jasmine was asleep. He climbed into bed and touched her gently to wake her. She opened her eyes and looked at him. "Did they sign the contracts?" she asked.

"They did. It is all finished and we can leave tomorrow."

"Oh, can we shop a bit before we go? Who knows when we will be in such a fine place as this again?" Jasmine had been thinking of this before she fell asleep and asked at once because she was not afraid of her husband.

John sighed and pretended to be troubled by this request. "Maybe those men are right," he said. "It is far more expensive to take a wife on a trip than to get a girl for one night."

But they both knew he would not deny her because he didn't like strange women as much as he liked Jasmine, and Jasmine was a good luck girl.

A LOW, WET ROOM

"It's one thing to suffer all my life,
but I don't want my sorrow to be lost.
I want people to know how I felt."
—Anonymous Nu Shu

It was on a day when I was being punished that I had the idea for telling my whole life story on a fan. The idea came to me because I discovered the fan – a beautiful shade of yellow, but empty of all decoration – in a terrible place: the place reserved for me whenever I fell out of favor with my husband's family.

My name is Ming and the room where I found the fan is the lowest room of my husband's house. It is so low that sometimes when we have a heavy rainfall there is water up to my ankles on parts of the floor. When the room gets wet like this it has a terrible, musty smell and ugly insects scurry up the walls to find a dry spot where they can rest.

The room has some shelves on one wall, high enough to be out of any water, and an old, creaky rocking chair that nobody wanted anymore. The chair is fairly comfortable but there is no way to put my feet up out of the water. And when the water comes it sometimes lasts for many days. So my feet get swollen from resting in the water and they hurt me. But sewing the story of my life into the fan makes me forget the pain in my feet. It helps to pass the time until they let me come out of the room and start to work again.

I can't remember any further back than the age of four, so that is where my story begins. In that year I was a happy child and I know I was happy all the time I lived at home. I was cared for by my family and not hated for being a girl. I already had friends who would become my sworn sisters and learn the Nu Shu with me when we were a little older. I did not have to work too hard for the family and there was always enough food so I was never hungry. I never heard my father complain that I was born a girl so I did not know that a girl's birth is an unhappy event for a family. Maybe it was because he already had sons or maybe it was because he was a generous man and did not mind providing for a girl. Whatever the reason, I always felt loved by him.

In the year I turned seven, with my feet already beautifully bound by my mother, I began to learn Nan Shu from my father. That is the men's writing, the writing known as Mandarin that is used by scholars and government officials and poets and philosophers. My father let me learn the real writing because he thought it was all right for girls to know how to write. At the same time my mother began teaching me Nu Shu, the women's writing, which all my sworn sisters were learning too. We had great fun practicing our sewing together, learning to make the Nu Shu symbols in stitches. My mother thought I would never need to use

Nu Shu because I was learning Nan Shu. But she wanted me to know it anyway, because all the women in our family had always learned it. And I wanted to know it because all my friends were learning to sew the symbols and it was fun to practice together and sing and talk.

When I was ten I already knew enough of the men's writing to write some little stories and to help my father keep the records of our household spending. My father let me study real books with real writing. He complimented me many times and said I was as smart as a boy. Sometimes my brothers teased me and said I knew too much for a girl, but they were mostly kind and I knew they loved me. Still, they cautioned me never to tell anyone outside our family that I knew the men's writing because maybe our father could get in trouble for teaching me. I never knew if that was true, but I didn't tell my girlfriends anyway. We were learning Nu Shu every afternoon together and sewing and laughing and telling stories, and I did not want to miss out on that. Girls sewing together is real life. It is true love. Girls understand each other because we all await the same fate: being removed to another home and becoming the servant of that family. It is a rare and lucky girl who finds true love in her marriage home.

When I was fifteen my family married me out to the Hsu family and I moved to Lonely River. My husband's mother and father were shocked when they realized I could read and write the men's writing. They said that to have a woman who can read and write in the house is bad luck. They told me that if they had known before the marriage that my father had taught me this they would never have wanted me for their son's wife. So maybe my brothers were right after all about not telling anyone. My mother-in-law decided that the only solution was to knock my head against the wall until I forgot all I knew. Most of the first year of my marriage I spent being beaten and having my head slammed against the wall until I was so dizzy and in so much pain that I did not talk about anything, much less the men's writing.

In my sixteenth year my husband's family decided that I must have lost all my men's knowledge and they found something to keep me busy that they thought was safe. They taught me how to make paper flowers and sent me out to the market to sell the flowers I made. When I was at home I was making flowers all day. Then I would go out and try to sell them. I liked being out at the market because I saw many beautiful things and a lot of people. But if I did not sell all my flowers my mother-in-law would beat me when I came home at night. So when I was at the market I began saying how beautiful the flowers were and using the most poetic language I knew to describe the beauty of the flowers so people would want to buy them. One day my father-in-law was in the market and he heard what I was saying. He said I obviously had not forgotten my learning if I could speak like that and he dragged me home and began to bang my head against the wall again. Then, for the first time, he put me in the low, wet room because he said hitting my head was not accomplishing anything.

So I stopped speaking entirely, at home or at the market.

When I was seventeen I received a set of napkins from one of my friends back home. On each napkin she sewed a story of a different woman from our village. One story moved me very much even though I could not remember, or maybe never knew, the woman she wrote about. This woman was a widow with three children, two boys and a girl. Her mother-in-law was still good to her and didn't blame her for the death of her son, because she was a widow, too, and knew how hard life can be. The napkin says they were raising the children together. One day they cut a small piece of cloth from the drapery behind their statue of Buddha and burned the cloth and dissolved the ashes in a cup of tea. They fed the tea to the children and hoped it would make them strong enough to face the hard world they were going to grow up in. But it made the children sick and one boy and the girl died. Now they have one boy left, but they are thankful for that because he is strong and can work and will eventually be the man they need to give them status. Even now, though he is only twelve years old, he can walk to market with them and give them permission to ride in a carriage or anything else they need to do. So their lives are not as barren as they might be if they had been left with no children or only the girl.

By the time I reached the age of eighteen I was very unhappy because I had already lost three babies and the whole family had decided that I was never going to be able to give them a son. This made my worth to them absolutely nothing. They kept me making and selling flowers and I did everything without speaking. I was afraid to risk a beating because I thought I might forget both the Nu Shu and the Nan Shu. But so far I had not forgotten anything.

I was also beaten and put in the room for other offenses, like cleaning too slowly or missing some dirt that everyone else saw or serving the dinner improperly. I began to understand that I could never please them, especially if I did not have a son because that was all they really wanted from me.

One day at the market I had been sitting on the ground for four hours and was feeling hungry and thirsty. The usual routine was for one of the children of the household to bring me some food at this time, but on this day nobody came. It was very hot and I was exhausted. I must have blacked out for a few moments because I found myself lying on the ground with several people staring down at me. As I began to open my eyes, everyone moved away except for one young man whom I recognized at once. He was Young Lion, one of the sons of my friend Lili. He had great kindness in his eyes and in his words. He asked if I felt all right and if I wanted some water from the stores of food and drink he was carrying to the stall of a friend of his across the road.

I knew I should not speak to him, much less accept his offer, but I was feeling so ill that I did, and he poured me a generous cup of water and handed me a slice of bread and an apple. He sat with me as I ate and drank and declared that my color was returning and that I would surely be fine. As he said those words I saw, from the corner of my eye, one of the children of my husband's brother standing in the road with a small package of food for me. His mouth was wide open and so were his eyes. As I motioned for him to come to me he turned and ran away, back toward the house. I suddenly felt even more ill than before I began to eat. I knew he was running home to tell everyone that I was sitting on the ground with a man. The fact that the young man was the son of my friend would not matter to anyone. They would never even listen to an explanation that would include that information. I would not have wanted to break my silence with them in order to give them an explanation. I expected that I would be punished in some way when I returned.

As it turned out, they did not wait for me to return. Within the hour my father-in-law was at the market gathering up all my unsold flowers and dragging me home. I wished I had waited for my food to be brought to me, but at the same time I resented that it was considered improper for me to accept help when I needed it.

I was beaten thirty strokes with a big stick. Then they locked me in the low room, which had recently been flooded after a big storm. The floor was damp and had some puddles of water here and there. My feet became swollen from the damp floor in just a few hours. I know they thought this would break me but it did not. Nothing they ever tried to do to me could break me.

When I was twenty my husband took a concubine and she gave him a son before the first year was over. Now the family was happier but they always found ways to remind me that I was not a good wife because I had not provided them with a son. I continued to sell flowers in the market and ever since the day I got so hungry and let Young Lion help me, I tried to steal a little piece of bread from the kitchen before I went out in the morning in case my food did not come in time. Then I knew I would have something to eat if I needed it. But still I lived in the low room with the water on the floor. They did not let me come out and join the rest of the family, except to work. The concubine slept with my husband so I slept in the low room.

Now I am in my twenty-fifth year. I live in my damp room when I am not at the market. I make flowers as fast as I can so I will be able to go often to the market. That is the only time I can go out into the fresh air so it is very important to me. Sometimes I ask the family for needle and thread and a piece of cloth so I can record my Nu Shu. This makes them think I am not too bad because it looks like I want to do women's work. But my feet are swollen from the water and my fingers are swollen also. I am always in pain. Still, even when I am feeling sick, I keep embroidering. I'm lucky my mother-in-law doesn't know Nu Shu, the way most of them do, so I can sew freely and I don't have to hide my work from her.

My plan was to write my life story, one segment of the fan for each year. This I have been doing, as anyone who has this fan can see. My story is embroidered in Nu Shu and I hope to find some way to get it back to one of my girlfriends from my old village. I don't believe anyone will take it for me now, but maybe much later, perhaps after I die, one of the young boys in the family will take the fan back for me. Some of them are growing up to be nice young men and may take pity on me when they are older. I hope there will still be someone alive who remembers me to receive the fan if that happens. I hope the sewing on this fan will speak for me because I have had to be silent so much of my life.

My feet and fingers swell more and become more painful every day. I wonder if swollen feet can kill a person. Sometimes I think my story is mostly told and it does not matter if I live any longer. What else will my life hold but more sewing, more flower making and more flower selling, and more swollen feet? I will never have a son so what purpose is there in my living any longer? Maybe this is what my husband's family thinks too, and they are hoping that I will die in this little damp room. Maybe I am hoping also.

But until I do I will continue to sew. I thank my father for teaching me Nan Shu and my mother for teaching me Nu Shu.

THE RED SKIRT

*"I married at thirteen and was
a widow at fourteen."*
—Anonymous Nu Shu

Rainy is huddled on a chair in the corner of the kitchen. It is the warmest corner of the whole house, but Rainy is shivering. She is sobbing, shaking with anger and sadness and the coldness of this late winter day, which has seeped into even this cozy corner of her home. But she is not making a sound – her sobs are silent – because she learned six years ago when her feet were being bound that a good girl does not cry. Rainy learned to cry silently. She is twelve years old now and her parents are close to making a marriage arrangement for her, but that is not what she is crying about, though it would be reason enough. She is crying because her mother has torn in half the beautiful red skirt that Rainy has been making for several weeks.

The sewing is flawless. The red skirt is covered with delicate white flowers, each one different from the others, maybe two dozen in all. Rainy worked on the skirt in secret because she wanted it to be part of her trunk of wedding clothes that she would bring to her new husband's family after the ceremony that united the two. At the last moment, though, as Rainy was cutting the last thread of the last flower, her mother entered her room and let out a scream that so frightened Rainy that she jumped up and let the skirt fall from her lap to the floor.

"You cannot wear that skirt. You cannot keep that skirt," her mother shouted. "White is the color of death. You will bring death to yourself and the whole family if you keep that skirt."

"But it is only the flowers," Rainy said. "The skirt itself is red, the color of good luck."

"That is no good. It is still too dangerous." She grabbed the skirt and ripped it down one of its perfect seams. "Now you destroy the rest," she said, "all of it. I do not want you even to use it as a cleaning rag."

Rainy's mother left the room and Rainy ran after her but nothing she could say would change her mother's mind. So finally Rainy was just able to sink down into the kitchen chair where now she sits and sobs. Her mother pokes her head back into the kitchen and says, "Someday you will see that this skirt is nothing. Only a mild disappointment. Life holds much harsher fates for women than losing a skirt. I hope your life is not difficult, but even the best lives are filled with loss. You will learn soon enough."

So Rainy rips and cuts and tears the skirt, amid crying and sighing and wishing life were different. She thinks of the husband choices her parents are right now debating and she doesn't like any of them. She thinks of the mothers of these boys, one of whom will become her mother-in-law, and doesn't look forward to living with them either. And she decides, just like that, when one half of the skirt is in shreds and one half is still a solid piece of cloth, that she isn't going to marry any of those boys and she isn't going to have any of their mothers for a mother-in-law because she isn't going to stay in her home and wait for it to happen.

Rainy leaves the shreds of half her skirt on the kitchen floor. The rest she takes to her room. She spreads it out on her bed and begins to put clothing on top of it. She adds a comb and her small mirror with the silver handle. Then she brings up the four corners of the cloth and ties them together making a small, neat bundle that she can carry in her arms. The family has a traveling trunk but it is too big and heavy for Rainy to manage on her own, so Rainy knows she will have to make do with this little package. She shoves the bundle under her bed and returns to the kitchen to clean. She will not be leaving her house until everyone is asleep and she wants to appear as normal as possible until that time.

While she is doing the cleaning that is expected of her this day, Rainy thinks about where she should go and what she will do when she gets there. She knows the women's secret language, but cannot read or write the men's language. Her feet were not bound properly so they are not as small as they should be, which is part of the reason – along with the poorness of the dowry her parents can provide – that her father is having a difficult time finding a match for her. But those big feet will make it possible for her to walk away from her fated marriage. A tea girl is probably the only job she can get, Rainy reasons, but even there, how desirable will she be without perfect feet?

Later that night, when all is quiet in the house and not even the leaves on the trees are stirring outside, Rainy gets up and pulls the bundle from under the bed. She uses the chamber pot and then walks through the kitchen on her way out. She sees her mother sitting in a corner asleep in her chair. Rainy's mother has been making a Third Day Book to give to Rainy when she marries. The book is open on her mother's lap. She has been working on it for several years now. It is all written in Nu Shu and explains to Rainy what she should expect when she gets married. Rainy knows this book and the marriage her mother plans for her both mean a lot to her mother. She feels a stab of guilt because the book will never be given to her. She imagines how her mother will feel when she realizes that Rainy is gone for good. Then she goes out of the house as quietly as she can.

The street outside is still. The afternoon winds have calmed and there is no dust. Rainy sets off for the next town where she knows a family that used to live in Lonely River. Her intention is to sleep beside their cottage and then ask for breakfast in the morning before she continues on to the next small town down the road where she thinks she will be able to find work in a tea house. Rainy has never been out walking at night and she is surprised at how dark it is, even with an almost-full moon. But she feels safer because of the darkness. If someone looks out the window of their house they will not be likely to notice her, she thinks. She keeps her head down and moves along and as she comes near to the center of town she notices the gourd she and her friends used in their seventh day of the seventh moon ceremony just lying on the ground under a tree. She is surprised to see it there as generally one of the girls keeps it, even though a new gourd will be used next time anyway.

Rainy pauses. The gourd looks so forlorn lying there unattended. She remembers the ceremony that has so recently taken place. All of her sworn sisters were there and each punched a hole in the gourd. Then, according to custom, they filled the gourd with water. As always, the water immediately started to leak through all the holes. This ceremony, performed once a year, helped them remind each other that they must keep the Nu Shu writing code a secret.

"If anyone tells about the Nu Shu," her sworn sister, Pink Melon, said, "it will be like the water leaking through the holes and the men will know. Each member of our group is responsible for keeping her mouth shut instead of letting the secret leak out. We keep our secrets and hide our embroidery."

Pink Melon hardly had to spell this out for them. They all knew that when one husband seems to begin to suspect something the wife will give her Nu Shu to another member to hide. Every member counts. If you leak the information it will affect everyone.

The ceremony is important but it is not the reason Rainy and her sworn sisters remember to keep the Nu Shu secret. They have been friends all their lives and learned the Nu Shu together. They know that whatever happiness they have depends on being able to write and sew Nu Shu together and alone, to meet and sing together, to keep their rituals and help and support each other. That is why they have a marriage cry when they learn that one of their number is going to be married. And why they sing sad songs for each other during a sworn sister's wedding. After they are married they will not depend on their husbands for happiness. They will barely know their husbands, sometimes not even meeting them until just before the wedding ceremony. Some of their husbands will be kind and some will not be. They know this will also be true of the mothers-in-law who will be running the households into which they move. Mostly they believe that as long as they have some contact with each other, even if only through the Nu Shu embroidered gifts they exchange, they will still have happiness together. But Rainy does not even believe that, and so she is leaving her dearest friends to escape her marriage, without knowing or caring who she will be betrothed to. She is that certain it will be a disaster.

Rainy thinks of her closest sworn sister, Beautiful Sunshine, who became her sworn sister because they were both born under the same sign. Their mothers are sworn sisters to each other and they prayed to the gods if one of them gave birth to a girl that the other one would, too, since the time of the births were to be so close. And their prayers were answered and the two girls became the closest of friends in the world. They learned the Nu Shu together, with Rainy's hand on her Auntie's hand and Beautiful Sunshine's hand on Rainy's. Together they wrote and sewed. Always together, their hands touching. Rainy knows the touch of Beautiful Sunshine's hand better than she knows her own, better than she will know her husband's if she ever has one.

"We have been the luckiest of girls," Rainy says out loud, even though she walks alone, "because we have always had each other. If I stayed in the village and we had daughters we would try to make them sworn sisters, just as we are."

But Rainy knows this can never happen now and she sighs as she thinks of Beautiful Sunshine and how she will feel when she learns that her best friend is gone. Will she understand why I had to leave, Rainy wonders. In her heart, Rainy knows her friend will be glad she got away but, still, sad to lose her forever.

As Rainy approaches a fork in the road she hears footsteps coming down the side road. It sounds like dozens of marching feet and that would mean dozens of men, for who else would be out at night? She sees a thicket of bushes a little way off to the side and runs to hide, settling in just in time to secure herself before the men arrive at the intersection and head down the same path Rainy was on. There are at least twenty men, maybe more. They seem to be about fifteen or twenty years old. They are marching very quickly, very close to each other, in lock-step fashion.

And then Rainy sees something that makes her stomach turn. Bile rushes up into her mouth and she tries to look away, but her eyes are glued to the sight. She sees that the reason the men are marching so closely to each other is that they are actually attached. Holes have been poked through their shoulders and a long chain has been run through the holes so that they are attached at the collar bones. Even in the darkness Rainy can see thin lines of blood running down their arms and backs.

She has heard stories about the army rounding up young men like this in villages, but she doesn't know much about the army or who is fighting whom. Now she sees it with her own eyes. These are not men, as she imagined, but boys, not much older than herself. These boys are doomed, she thinks. She has heard that if they try to escape from service and are captured they will have their heads chopped off. To see what a sorry sight they are, bloody and bedraggled, she does not doubt it for a moment. She wonders when they have eaten last and thinks that sometimes the lot of men is not that much better than that of women. Certainly not men who have been dragged into the army this way.

Another thought comes to her: that wherever these boys are being taken there will be employment for tea girls. And maybe these young men, after all they have been through, will not be so particular about the size of a woman's feet. So she decides to follow them, at a safe distance, and possibly find the town where her future is waiting.

It is a long night for Rainy and just as the sky is beginning to brighten she sees an encampment ahead. It is not the village of her friends but, rather, an army base of some sort. She does not know where she is, if she has passed her friends' village in the night or just gone in a different direction while following the men, or maybe not even reached the village yet. Truly, she is too tired to care. She ducks behind a tree, sets her red bundle down on the ground and lies down, using the bundle as a pillow. Within minutes she is asleep.

But she does not sleep for long. Not even until the sun is fully up – maybe two or three hours at most. She wakes up feeling she is not alone. And, indeed, she is not. A tall soldier stands above her, looking down at her with a question in his eyes. He is young, but not as young as the boys she saw earlier, chained together at their necks.

"Girl," he says, "why are you here? This is no place for girls. This is an army encampment, the great army of Mao Zedong. You must move along at once or you will be in much trouble. Or you can come back when you are older. In Mao's army women can serve as well as men."

As he speaks, Rainy realizes that her plans have collapsed. She does not know where she is, she does not know how to find the home of her friends. She has no food and no place to go. And that includes going home; she can never go back there because, having stayed out alone overnight, she is now a ruined woman in the eyes of her family and of the town. There is no way her parents will ever be able to marry her out now. And she does not understand anything about women serving in an army as not much news about Mao has reached the little village of Lonely River.

"I am going to be a tea girl when I find a place to work in some town," Rainy tells the soldier, with as much confidence as she can muster.

He laughs. "A tea girl, you say? If that's what you want, you can be a tea girl right here. You are too far to walk to any town, but we have a tea house right here on the base for the officers. And maybe when we move the camp they will let you come with us. Many of the tea girls do that."

Rainy drops her head. This is a big decision and she has no idea what to do.

"I am hungry," she whispers and the young soldier laughs again. "Come to the tea house, then. They will feed you and see if you are fit to be a tea girl for this army. But if not," he glances at her feet and shakes his head, "you will have to go on. Maybe back to your family. You are very young."

"How can I ever go back now that I have spent the night here?" Rainy asks. "And I don't want to. I will be a tea girl here, or somewhere else."

The soldier shakes his head again. "Come along then. Follow me."

Rainy picks up her red bundle and the two walk a short way down the path until they come to a small cabin. Rainy can see that it has been constructed hastily and will be easy to abandon when the army moves on. All the buildings, she notices now, seem to be of shoddy construction, but some are quite large, probably barracks for the men to sleep in. Few men are walking around and

Rainy wonders what they are all doing and how many there are.

"In here." The young soldier motions for Rainy to follow him into the cabin. Inside are two small tables, each occupied by three men sipping tea and joking with each other. The room becomes silent when Rainy enters. A plain-looking girl stands at a back room door and Rainy feels a rush of relief to see another female in the room.

"New tea girl for you if you want," the soldier says to the girl. "Big feet, but pretty face. Seems agreeable. Up to you. I can send her on her way if you prefer."

The room goes quiet.

The girl at the door, who Rainy figures to be pretty old, close to twenty maybe, frowns a bit. "I'll talk to her. We'll see. Sit her down over there and give her something to drink. Water. And thanks for bringing her in. I expect we can use her."

She barks out her orders without a trace of a smile and impatiently pushes her dull hair behind her ears. The soldier guides Rainy to a seat and places a cup of water in front of her. He gives a slight bow to the mistress of the establishment, and leaves before Rainy can even thank him. She wishes he had given her some food too, and wonders if she dare ask for something. But before she can decide, the girl in charge is bending down and putting her face right up to Rainy's.

"Let me see your feet," the girl says. "Big. You won't fetch much, even from these guys. Once I take my cut you won't have but a pittance left for yourself. Are you sure you want to be a tea girl?"

"I don't want to marry," Rainy says. "I want to be independent."

The older girl lets out a roar of laughter. The men at the closer table snicker. "Well, you'll never marry, you can be sure of that. But you'll not make enough with those feet to be independent, either. You think this is better than marriage?"

"I don't want a mother-in-law who beats me."

When Rainy says that everyone in the cabin laughs. They are all enjoying this conversation. One of the men at the closer table makes his hand into a fist and slams it down on a plate in front of him, breaking the plate. He stands quickly and turns to Rainy.

"You have a preference, then, as to who beats you? You are a discerning young woman. You prefer to be beaten by a soldier than by a mother-in-law. I wish you all the luck in the world. You have made your choice. There is no turning back for you. It's too bad your mother did not do a better job with your feet. Their appearance alone will invite your first beating. I would give it to you myself but I have already spent my money. Maybe some other time."

And with that he leaves the cabin, laughing all the way out the door. Rainy looks around and sees the life she has chosen. And knows there is no turning back. She touches her travel bag made of the red skirt with the white flowers, which has been lying at her feet all this time. And takes a sip of water.

PART FOUR — 1950

BIG FEET

"We embroider a thousand patterns.
Younger brother reads a thousand books."
—Anonymous Nu Shu

Coral sat on a chair in her bedroom and looked at her feet, much as her sister Lili had done more than twenty years earlier. But what she saw was very different. Not the tiny three-inch feet her sister saw back on the day she went to visit her mother, but big, ugly, foreign-type feet. No lotus shape in the soles of her feet. No delicate little embroidered slippers for her.

Coral's feet had not been bound. There were many reasons for this. She had no mother because her mother had died when she was born. And, really, only a mother could face the agony of inflicting pain on her child even when it was for her own good. When she was two, Coral's sister Lili came and took her from her father. Lili was the best big sister in all the world. Just like a beloved mother. But Lili said it was against the law to bind little girls' feet. She said it had been outlawed all the way back in 1911, long before Coral was born. And Lili was smart and must be right. But still. Every girl Coral knew had bound feet – her age, older, younger, they all had beautiful little lotus-shaped feet that the men loved. And sure enough, here she was, twenty-two years old and not married. No man in Lonely River wanted a wife with big, ugly feet – feet like the kind foreign women have.

As Coral pondered her big feet that afternoon, her mind turned to a secret she had. It was something else that made her different from other women, but it was something that was not visible to the eyes of everyone she met in the way her big feet were. She thought back to when she was six years old and one of Lili's sons, who would technically be her nephew even though he was older than Coral by almost eight years, was playing a parlor game with her to while away the hours of a cold winter evening. No one else was paying attention when he whispered to her "Do you want me to show you how to read?"

Coral was shocked. She knew that only men could read. She knew already that women had a secret code and she was learning to sew it. But men read the real language and that she knew nothing about.

"Come here. I'll show you," Young Lion, her nephew, whispered, his dark eyes sparkling with mischief.

"Is it okay to show me?"

"Don't tell," he said. "I'll show you everything, but don't tell."

Coral huddled up close to Young Lion and he showed her the book he did his lessons in. The first thing she noticed was that the symbols were something like the Nu Shu symbols she was learning to sew, but she didn't say a word about that. Lili had told her many times that Nu Shu was a secret for women only and she must never tell a man how it works. She wondered for a moment if since Young Lion was sharing the men's writing with her he might ask her to show him the women's writing. But she was pretty sure that Young Lion didn't even know there was a women's writing, so she just kept quiet the way Lili always said she should.

After that night Young Lion showed Coral the men's writing every chance he had. Coral loved learning to read it. She learned that it was the language of business in China and it was called Mandarin. She learned to read it pretty well over time and to write it, too. She never told anyone, not even Lili, that Young Lion was teaching her. She could not risk sharing the secret with anyone because if someone found out what Young Lion was doing, the first thing that would happen would be that he would never teach her again. And Coral loved Mandarin. She wanted to learn all she could of it. Nu Shu was more beautiful, but Mandarin, she felt, was more important. Because men used it, of course, but also because there were so many stories written in this language and Coral wanted to read them all.

After a while Coral was able to read some of the stories in Young Lion's other books, and soon she began to write the symbols on papers Young Lion brought her from his school. She kept all her writing at the bottom of her clothes drawer and she knew that it must never be seen by anyone. Coral had heard a story from Lili about a woman whose father taught her to read Mandarin. When she married she told her husband that she could read the men's writing. He told his mother and together they decided that they could not keep her because it was bad luck to have a woman in the house who could read. They beat her and sent her back to her parents. And Coral, like all the women in the village, knew the story of Ming, who had been so brutally treated by her husband's family, and kept for days on end in their wet basement, in the hopes that she would forget the Mandarin she had learned from her father. So Coral had good reason to keep her knowledge a secret, but she wished sometimes that she could at least tell Lili. She didn't dare, though, if only because it would put Lili in danger if she knew.

Now Coral began to wonder what she would do with the rest of her life since she was sure she would never marry. Lili's sons, her nephews, were all married now and their wives did most of the work. The family could manage without her and no one would care if she left, except that Lili would be sad. But Lili always said Coral could have a real job because her feet were big enough to walk on.

And there were big changes happening in the country now that Chairman Mao was the Great Leader. Laws about land were changing and so were marriage laws. Young Lion showed her a newspaper one day that said that a man and a woman both have to consent in order for a marriage to take place. A girl cannot be forced anymore. But still, all the marriages Coral knew about were arranged, so it was clear people were not following the new laws in Lonely River.

Practically everyone knew that foot binding was outlawed

now. Some people still did it, but it was going to stop everywhere in the future, she was sure of that. The biggest new ruling was that girls could go to school. Chairman Mao said men and women are equal – Coral had read that in the newspaper but she could hardly believe it. Men and women equal? Would boys and girls learn the same things in school, including how to read Mandarin? It didn't seem possible. Girls with big feet like hers all over the place? Going to school? Well, they would have to have big feet in order to be able to walk to school with the boys. Maybe then she could admit she knew how to read the men's writing without getting herself and Young Lion in trouble. Maybe. Someday.

While Coral was imagining herself telling the world she could read Mandarin, and trying to picture what it might be like choosing her own husband and making her own decision to marry, Young Lion came rushing into her bedroom.

"Excuse me, Auntie," he said with his usual sly smile, "but I've just received the most interesting news. Central Hospital in Ji'an has just opened a training program for girl hospital nurse-assistants. They will teach girls to read Mandarin and how to assist nurses in caring for patients. I think you should do this. And you already know how to read. You'll be a star pupil from the first day."

Coral did not move. Could not move, in fact. Just when she had been thinking about what to do with her life, along comes this opportunity. But how could she go away by herself?

"How would I get there?" she asked when she could find her

voice again. "And where would I live?"

"There are dormitories for the students. And after you finish your studies you would get a job at the hospital and you could afford to pay for your own apartment."

"But what would Lili say?"

"I think my mother would be happy to see you do this," Young Lion said. "I would take you to Ji'an myself. I hope you'll think about it."

Coral did little else but think about it. While doing her chores, while sewing her Nu Shu, even in her dreams at night, she was studying at the hospital and working at the hospital. She thought about living in a dormitory and then living alone in her own apartment. About all the people she would meet. Would the other women have bound feet? Maybe at the hospital she would find other women with big feet like hers. Other women who could read too, since they would all have to learn. It felt like going to another country, another planet. Everything would be different from anything she had ever known.

Coral thought about their neighbor Pearl and how she had lived alone until she met the man who was traveling through Lonely River. Coral and Lili were there when she met him. He left, but then a few weeks later he came back. And every time he traveled he stopped at Pearl's cottage. And one day Pearl announced that she and the man were getting married, even though they had both been married before. Lots of people in the town whispered about Pearl having two husbands but nobody stopped them from getting married and after a time people seemed to forget that they hadn't been man and wife forever.

What would people say if Coral decided to go to Ji'an to study? The Great Leader himself said men and women are equal. Since men can go and study anywhere or anytime they want to, that means women can too, she reasoned. So what difference did it make what anyone whispered about her behind her back? She was lucky to have big feet and she was beginning to realize that. They'd been laughing at her and her big feet all her life. Well, now the laugh was on them. They're stuck in Lonely River, she thought, and I can get out.

So Coral took the plunge. She told Young Lion she was going to go to the hospital school and she told Lili and slowly everyone in the village found out. If they laughed at her she didn't know. And if she knew, she didn't care. Young Lion drove her to Ji'an in his new car – he was the first man in the village to get one – and everyone came out to wave goodbye and wish her well. It was hardest to say goodbye to Lili but she knew she wasn't leaving forever and Lili knew that too. She held Lili long and close in a tight hug and whispered in her ear, "Thank you," and Lili knew Coral was thanking her for everything: for taking her from her father's house where there was no room for her, for raising her and teaching her Nu Shu, for looking the other way when she must have known Young Lion was teaching her Mandarin because Lili knew everything that went on in the house. But most of all, for not binding her feet. And Lili knew at last, for sure, that she had made the right decision about Coral's feet, that Coral would walk away from Lonely River and have a real life of her own. Maybe she would never marry, it's true, but maybe there were men in the big city who were looking for more in a woman than tiny feet and a sexy walk and maybe Coral would meet one of them.

. . . .

Coral closed her books and stretched. She was due at the hospital in twenty minutes and she couldn't wait to get there. She didn't mind studying and found that most of what she had to learn came fairly easily to her. But her favorite part of her training was the actual work in the hospital. She loved everything about it. She liked the doctors and the nurses and she liked the patients. Now that she was into her nurse-assistant training she was pretty sure she was going to go on and study to be a real nurse. She was a natural at cleaning bedpans and changing linens and couldn't wait until she would learn to clean wounds and change dressings. Two of her teachers had already told her that she should continue her studies and become a nurse.

Another thing Coral liked about her training was that there were lots of women, from all over the province, who did not have tiny feet. She never would have imagined that so many girls of her age had not had their feet bound, but outside her village and the surrounding villages there were many mothers who, in fact, had not bound their daughters' feet. For the first time in her life, Coral felt comfortable with other women. It was a good feeling to be like everyone else.

Coral grabbed her books and ran out the door. The hospital was right across the street from her dormitory and she arrived just on time. The day always started with visiting patients and Coral checked the assignment list to see which ward she was supposed to go to. Then off she went, never forgetting to appreciate her big feet and her sister Lili because without Lili she would not be in this wonderful place that she loved so much.

The first patient on her list was new – a man just admitted that morning. She read the description: broken hip and concussion. Maybe a car accident, she thought as she walked over to the bed. The ward was dark and the man was asleep. The patients in the other occupied beds were quiet also. Her patient was quite thin and covered up to his neck. His face was smooth and his hair thick and dark – probably in his thirties, she thought. She watched him for a few moments but he didn't move so she went on to the other patients on her list.

There was a young girl with leukemia whom she had been visiting for several days; she stayed a while with her and the two played a card game until the nurses came to take the girl downstairs for tests. Then she went to visit an elderly man who needed some help with eating and she fed him his lunch. Two more patients on the list and she was ready to go to her first class.

When classes were over, Coral was free to return to her dormitory room to study, or visit her patients again. Usually she liked to go home and get right to her books, but today she wanted to see the new patient and meet him if he was awake. She never liked to miss talking to each of her patients. So she returned to his ward and found him still lying in bed, but very much awake.

"Mr. Chow," she said, "I see you are awake."

He looked at her. "Very much so," he said. "How could I be otherwise with the noise coming from my companions here."

Coral looked over at the other beds. The three men were talking to each other, but they weren't terribly loud. "Your concussion may have made you sensitive to noise."

"I see you are a doctor," Mr. Chow said with just the slightest sneer.

"Oh, no. I am just a nurse-assistant in training," said Coral. "But I am going to be a real nurse eventually when I finish my studies."

"Ah," said Mr. Chow, "what a surprise. I was sure you were a doctor." The sneer became a bit more pronounced and Coral knew he was making fun of her.

"I see your water glass is almost empty," she said. "Let me refill it for you."

He reached out his arm as if to stop her and then drew it back. "If you want to," he said. She saw that his left hand was missing its last finger and had a scar besides. She took the glass and filled it.

"Would you like to tell me how you broke your hip?" she asked when she returned with the filled water glass.

"Not particularly," he said. "Nor would I like to tell you how I got this concussion or how I lost my finger or how I got this scar or why when my hip is healed and I get up and walk I will be limping because I was already limping before the accident. No, I would not like to tell you any of that because it isn't any of your business."

Coral lowered her eyes to the floor. "I'm sorry," she said. "I'll leave now. But I'll be back tomorrow. I hope I can be of some help to you then. I'm just learning my job, you see."

She turned and left, silently asking herself why she had bothered to say all that. The men in the other beds were laughing and she realized that sometime during the conversation they had grown silent and were listening. "Well, let them," she thought, "I haven't done anything wrong. It's Mr. Chow who is rude. Maybe he'll feel better tomorrow."

An image of his scar popped into her head and she wondered what it would feel like if she touched it and just as quickly wondered why such a thought would ever occur to her. She'd seen many scars. Why would she think of touching this one?

The next morning Coral awoke thinking of Mr. Chow. Maybe she had dreamed about him but, if so, she didn't remember. She thought she'd go to see him first, just to find out if a night's sleep had put him in a better mood.

When she entered his room he was sitting up in a chair and eating his breakfast. He looked slimmer than she imagined he was, and taller, too. Now that she could see his entire body in a more normal position she found him rather attractive with a serious, thoughtful face, not unkind-looking at all.

"Ah, my nurse-assistant has arrived," he said. "Have you come here to feed me? As you can see, I am doing quite well without your attention."

"I've just come to see how you're feeling and mark it in my chart. It's a requirement. How are you feeling?" She waved the chart quickly in front of his face by way of demonstration.

He laughed. "And I thought you really cared about me."

Coral's face went red. She did not know how to have this sort of light conversation with men. Even in the hospital things were kept on a rather formal level. And she rarely got to know anyone very well as they moved on to other wards for one reason or another, or went home and were then out of her life as quickly as they'd come into it.

"Well, I do care of course. You are one of my patients so I care very much how you're doing. And I'm happy to see that you look quite cheerful this morning as compared to yesterday afternoon. I hope that means you are not in pain."

"Not in much pain," he answered and turned his attention to the half-eaten eggs on his plate. Coral felt that she was meant to leave now but she didn't want to go just yet. Still, she had a list of patients to see and not that much time before classes. She should be moving along and see how the others were doing.

Mr. Chow looked up at her. "What else do you want to know?"

"I'd like to know how you got all those other injuries you mentioned yesterday."

The words, as they came out of her mouth, were as much a surprise to Coral as they were to Mr. Chow. She couldn't believe she'd said them. He would probably tell her again that it was none of her business, she thought, and truly it was not.

But, instead, he laughed. "You are very persistent. Do you need the information for that chart of yours?"

"No, I'm sorry. I shouldn't have asked again."

Another laugh. "Okay," he said, "I give up. If you come back this afternoon and if I'm awake I'll tell you about the other injuries. It will be a good lesson to you. You'll be sorry you asked. They are not pretty stories for girls to hear. But then you are no ordinary girl, I can see. You are a nurse-assistant. And soon to be a nurse. You'll have to get the stomach for it sometime, so maybe now is the time."

Coral was pretty sure he was making fun of her again, but she didn't care. She was unaccountably happy to have an excuse to come back and see Mr. Chow again and sit and talk for a time, not just step in and out and make a mark on her list of patients. The other men in the other beds were listening once more, but it didn't matter to her now.

Later, as she was leaving her class, her professor called her name.

"Coral. One moment, please."

She stopped and turned. "Yes, sir?"

"I want to discuss your last exam with you."

Coral would have loved to say she was in a hurry and could

they do that tomorrow, but she didn't dare. Actually, the news was good. Her grade was so high that her professor was recommending her for nursing training in the very next quarter, sooner than Coral had dared to hope for.

She thanked him and he said, "I would like to take you out for coffee so we can discuss your training and how you should prepare. You're my star pupil and I'm going out on a limb to recommend you so early. I want to be sure you are ready and do not cause me to lose face after I have told everyone how clever you are."

Coral did not want to have coffee with this man. She wanted to see Mr. Chow and hear the stories about all his injuries. But of course she could not say that. She could not say anything, but just nodded her agreement and followed the professor out the door.

"Professor Gao," she said when they were seated in the hospital cafeteria, "I really can't stay very long. I want to visit my patients again today."

"Nonsense," he said. "You've seen them already. It's good that you're so attentive, but it's not necessary to see them twice a day. This is much more important. We have to map out a strategy for your education. When you are a nurse you will be seeing your patients all day long. Right now your studies are your priority."

He glanced at his wrist. "Look at the time. I'll order us some noodles. We might as well have dinner."

Professor Gao kept Coral at the table for two hours. She knew he was right about her priorities and she was fascinated by his talk of nursing school and his suggestions for extra work she should do to prepare for her training. She loved studying and was very pleased with herself for doing so well that she was being singled out in this way. She even thought about how proud and happy Lili would be when she heard the news. But in the back of her mind was Mr. Chow and his promise of stories. When Professor Gao finally released her it was already dark and she almost ran to Mr. Chow's room.

When she got there he was asleep, as she feared he might be. All the men seemed to be asleep. She moved around a bit and made little noises, but no one stirred. Mr. Chow's left arm was resting on top of the covers and she had the strangest impulse to touch the long scar that ran from his knuckles to his elbow, but she didn't dare. Oh, how she wanted to hear the story of that scar, but it was not to be tonight.

. . . .

In less than two years, Coral received her nursing certificate in a wonderful ceremony that Lili and Young Lion attended. She introduced them to Professor Gao and told them how helpful he had been to her all through her years of study. Professor Gao, for his part, could not have been prouder of Coral if she had been his own child. They all celebrated afterward with coffee in the hospital cafeteria.

Lili stayed on for two days with Coral in her apartment. She helped Coral buy new clothes for her nursing job which was to start the very next week in the same hospital. Lili told Coral all the news of the village. The biggest news was that the concubine, Star Angel, had risen in status to such a degree in her home that her master had allowed her to have surgery on her eyes and they weren't crossed anymore. Coral asked about Pearl and her husband and Lili told her that they were doing well despite being quite aged. They helped each other in their little garden and had a nice, peaceful life.

Coral told Lili that she had only one regret. That she had met a nice man among her patients when she was a student. She was meant to go back and visit with him again but her studies delayed her and when she was able to return he was asleep. She told Lili of Mr. Chow's injuries and how he had promised to tell her the stories behind all of them. When she did get back the next day he had already been released from the hospital and no one could tell her where he went. She thought of him often and hoped he didn't think that she had just forgotten about him.

Lili asked Coral about one of Mr. Chow's injuries, the scar on his arm. She told Coral that once when she was little more than a baby they had met a boy who had a scar on his arm and who had helped retrieve a goose that had been stolen from the concubine, Star Angel.

"You were very interested in that scar," she said, "and you touched it. He was a nice boy and said it was all right for you to touch it. I guess you have always been interested in scars. You must have been meant to be a nurse from very early in life."

"What was the boy's name?" Coral asked. "Did he ever say, or did you ask him?"

"I think it was Tiger," Lili said. "Yes, Tiger. I remember now, he made much of it. He said his family had named him Tiger Boy but he had outgrown that name and was going into the army or something like that. This must have been some twenty years ago. I can't imagine why I still remember, but he was such a nice young boy."

"I wonder how Mr. Chow got his scar. I wanted to touch his scar too, but I didn't dare. Of course, I'm not a little baby any more. How funny that I would want to do that."

"Well, maybe you'll meet your Mr. Chow again someday," said Lili.

And maybe she would, thought Coral. But first she had to start being a nurse. That was to begin the very next day and Coral simply could not wait. Before Lili left for home that afternoon, Coral thanked her again for not binding her feet. And Lili told her how much she had struggled with the decision and how relieved she was that she had made the right one.

"Where would I be now if I had tiny, broken feet? Oh, Lili, I shudder to think of it. You have given me a life two times – once when you brought me to your home and again when you didn't bind my feet. Three times, really, because you let Young Lion teach me Mandarin. I know now that you must have known he was doing it."

"I thought if you were going to work it would help you and

I'm so glad I was right. You are well launched, Coral. You are going to do well in the world. And I am going to leave now so you can begin your life as a nurse. Think of me, Coral, and visit me when you can."

The sisters kissed and Lili left. Coral knew the feeling of having her whole life before her, and the excitement of knowing she really wanted to do what she was going to do. And so her life as a nurse began.

And Lili, too, was content. She knew she had done the best she could for her sister. Though she didn't know all of what the future held for China she was sure that Coral was going to be just fine in the new world that China was becoming. Still, she could not possibly have anticipated the assault that was waiting to be launched upon their beloved Nu Shu linens, or the part Coral was to play in preserving the stories of some of the women of Lonely River.

PART FIVE — 1967

— P A R T   F I V E - 1 9 6 7 —

SAVING NU SHU

THE POMEGRANATE
"The flowers of the pomegranate are red as fire
My heart is burning like the hottest fire
in the world.
Fortunate is the pomegranate,
which is allowed to bloom
Unfortunate am I who is never allowed to bloom.
The world will know the brilliant color
of the pomegranate
The world will never know
the passion that is mine.
The pomegranate will drop its petals and feel its
color in the memory's eye of many viewers.
And I will also die and all my passion
will fade away.
My passion will never become a fruit like the flower
of the pomegranate will.
Nor will the world ever remember a woman's
passion that has never had a chance to bloom."
—Anonymous Nu Shu

Coral held the fragment of the poem in her hands and read it over and over. It was embroidered around the edges of a shawl meant to keep a woman warm on winter nights. It was not something she had written nor was it written by her sister Lili. It might have been the work of one of Lili's daughters-in-law but she doubted it. More likely, one of the daughters-in-law was hiding it for a friend whose husband had discovered the Nu Shu secret and threatened to destroy her work.

A sigh escaped Coral's lips. So much Nu Shu could not be identified. So much was missing. Sometimes she could tell by reading the stories who had sewn a particular item, but not always. Lili and her daughters-in-law had hidden many beloved embroidered Nu Shu items over the years for as many different reasons. Now it was hard to sort it all out with so many people moving about, often for jobs, not always because they wanted to. And so many houses ransacked during the Cultural Revolution that had China by its throat, as the authorities tried to destroy everything created in the China of old.

Tiger poked his head in the door of the living room of their small apartment in Ji'an and Coral smiled. She always smiled when she saw him, though he was a very serious man. So serious that when she first met him in the hospital she knew him only as Mr. Chow. He never told her the rest of his name was Tiger, not that that would have reminded her of her very first meeting with him because she was so young then that no memory survived.

This time Tiger smiled back, probably because Coral looked

so small sitting amid piles of tablecloths, napkins and fans, all embroidered with Nu Shu stitches.

"I'm making tea," he said. "Would you like some?"

"Yes, thanks. And Tiger, would you look at this? It's an item I couldn't identify until all of a sudden it struck me what it was."

She held up a long, narrow strip of cloth covered with Nu Shu sewing. "No idea," he said. "What is it?"

"I think it's a foot binding cloth," Coral said. "But it was never used. It would have blood and other stains on it if it had been used. It would be wrinkled and dirty. Maybe the mother made it for her daughter but the daughter didn't live. Or maybe she made it for her baby before the baby was born and then it turned out to be a boy. Then she saved it for another child but she never had a girl. It tells the story of the hopes the mother has for the little girl's life."

"Wicked," Tiger said, "breaking children's feet like that. I'm glad that never happened to you."

"You wouldn't even know me if it did. I would never have become a nurse and I would never have met you in the hospital – would not have met you twice, in fact."

"That's true. But don't forget you met me three times before we really got to know each other. Remember when you were a baby?"

"No. Of course I don't remember. But I know the story is true because you and Lili remember. And I even asked Star Angel and she remembers. Everyone except me knows that I touched your scar when I was two years old and you rescued Star Angel's goose from the man who grabbed it. Not much must have ever happened in Lonely River if everyone remembers that little story."

"I don't suppose much did," Tiger said. "I was just passing through. On my way to the army."

Coral shuddered. She always felt a strange sense of relief when she thought about Tiger going into the army at the age of twelve. Of course they would take anyone then, boy or man. The relief she felt was because he had come through it alive and found his way back to her. With a broken hip, broken leg, shot off finger, concussion, even a bullet that was still lodged deep in his shoulder. But alive. A woman he didn't know he was looking for. And a man she didn't know she had lost. Not that their story was singular in a China torn by internal strife. But it had a happy ending because they did find each other again.

Sometimes when they sat on the sofa together and read, or snuggled up in bed, Coral would trace Tiger's scar with her fingers and Tiger would always say it felt just the same as when she was two years old. And Coral would always say, "I don't remember but I believe you." And then they would kiss and hold each other tight because they knew how easily it could have happened that they would never have found each other again.

"So what are you going to do with all this stuff?" Tiger asked when they were sitting together and drinking their tea. "We can't just keep it forever. We don't have room for it."

"I know," said Coral. "I don't know what to do with it. I have to get it to a safe place. The women protected the Nu Shu all their lives. I can't let it go to the government authorities now. They think it's art from the old days and they want to destroy it. And it is art. But it's people's lives, too. It's all the women's stories. We can't let them fall into the wrong hands."

"Just remember," said Tiger, always the careful and practical one, "you could wind up in jail if they find you hiding this. And I wouldn't be able to get you out. It would be horrible. It's not worth risking your life for it."

A dark look came over Coral's face. "Women risked their lives many times to save their stories. I can do no less. I will find a way to save it all for Lili's sake and Pearl's and Star Angel with her crooked stitches, for all of them."

Outside the apartment there was suddenly a huge commotion. They ran to the window and saw what they'd seen before too many times: books and paintings being thrown on a huge bonfire.

"Right on our street it's happening," Tiger said. "I'm furious. This is not what I fought for. If they come to our apartment we are going to lose the Nu Shu. They'll grab it up in a minute, and the fire is already burning. It will be so easy to toss it all into the fire."

And then it happened, as they knew it would. A knock at the door. They weren't even surprised.

"Authorities. Open up," loud and clear from the hallway.

Coral and Tiger looked at each other and, reluctantly, he moved toward the door. Coral began shoving everything she could under the sofa, but there were still many piles of embroidered fabric around. She kicked them in every direction and tried to make it look like a housekeeping mess.

"Open, I said."

"Coming."

Tiger opened the door. Two men were standing there. "Tiger!" one called out. Tiger looked at their faces and knew immediately that one was an old army buddy.

"Wow," he said. "Swift Wind. I never thought I'd see you again in this life. I can't believe you wound up here in Ji'an. Hey, it's great to see you again."

The second man pushed them both aside and stepped in the door. "Inspection for antiques," he said.

"Just a minute," Swift Wind said to his partner. "I haven't seen this guy in a long time. I'm surprised he's even alive, the scrapes he got himself into. You should hear some of his stories."

"Some other time, buddy. We've got a job to do. And lots of apartments to look at. Let's get moving here." He shoved Swift Wind into the apartment and followed behind him, pushing Tiger aside at the same time. He was tall and menacing and, though Tiger was not afraid of many people, this guy made him feel threatened. He glanced over at Coral, who was standing still and quiet on the other side of the room. He tried to give her a look of confidence but he knew she knew the score and wouldn't be fooled into thinking he was in control.

"Listen, fellas," Tiger said. "My wife is silly, but she's embarrassed about the mess. She begs you to give her time to clean up. We don't have anything you'd want anyway, but I know you have to look. Could you do our apartment last? Give her a little time to clean up? It would make me a hero, I can tell you."

The men chuckled knowingly. "Women," the other man said. "They're all the same. But this is men's business, not women's. In fact it's the business of the state, as you well know. We can't be making appointments here. Move aside now."

"Oh, come on," Swift Wind said, "This guy fought right beside me, I tell you. He's okay. It's no big deal. We can come back on our way out. But no one can leave the building, even empty-handed, till we finish our inspection of all the apartments. If the guards see her running out the back they'll shoot on sight. It won't matter that we once served side by side, Tiger."

"I get it. No, don't worry. She isn't going anywhere. Neither am I. She just wants to straighten the place up. Thank you. Thank you."

The other man, whose name remained unknown to Tiger, glared at Swift Wind. "Who do you think you are, changing the rules? I don't care who this guy is. You're just giving them a chance to hide something. I'll bet they've got an old jade ring under the cushions of the couch. I'll report you if you persist in this. Inspections are random. We don't let people set their own time."

"It's a small thing. I want to do a favor for a friend. Tiger never had anything of value in his life. Look at this apartment. He still doesn't have anything of value. You can see that. Let it go. Or maybe I need to make a report to the authorities about where you were last night."

The menacing face of the other soldier turned white for a moment, and then red. His right hand wrapped itself into a fist, but he thought better of it when Swift Wind did the same.

"What the hell," he said. "Who cares? Have it your way." He looked directly at Tiger and said, "We're talking about twenty minutes. We'll be back so fast you won't believe it."

The men backed out the door and Tiger shut it.

"We don't have much time. They tear through people's apartments in minutes, grabbing anything they even suspect is art of the old. What do you think we should do?"

Coral was standing in the middle of the room, weeping now.

"Stop that. It won't help and you're wasting time."

Coral stopped at once. Tiger was there to help her. She could do it. She had to do it. "Take the bedcovers off the bed and the cases off the pillows. Stuff the pillows under the bed." She had suddenly taken command.

She rushed to gather up the tablecloths and folded as many of them as she dared carefully over the bed. Then she put the bedcovers over them. The bed looked a little more luxurious, perhaps, but not too overly stuffed. The napkins she placed in the pillow cases and tried to make them look as much like real pillows as she could. "The guards are all men," she thought, "with luck they won't look too carefully at the appearance of a bed."

There were some shawls and she draped them over the sofa, embroidered parts carefully folded under, and hoped the men would not remember that they weren't there before. They will have seen a number of other apartments before they return, she reasoned, and they didn't get much of a look at ours before they left.

"Perhaps we can lay the fans out carefully beneath the cushions of the sofa," Tiger said. "As long as we don't actually sit down on them, they'll be all right." He set about doing that but Coral stopped him.

"You heard what they said about a ring hidden in the sofa cushions. They'll look there for sure. I know. Let's put them in the refrigerator. Maybe they won't look in there." Tiger looked skeptical but Coral began to shove the fans into the small refrigerator in the corner of their tiny kitchen. To the collection of fans Coral added one old coin that Lili had found in her mother's drawer and passed on to Coral. She wasn't sure if it was valuable or not, but it dated back to 1860 and was produced during the Taiping Rebellion. It had Nu Shu writing imprinted on it, and although Coral didn't know what the symbol meant, she considered it as important as any other Nu Shu artifacts she possessed.

When they were finished, Coral had but one item left: the binding cloth for the little girl. She held it in her hands almost reverently. It was, possibly, the most precious of all the items to her because its story held the hopes of all mothers in the China of old – that by breaking their little girls' feet they were ensuring them a secure future. And though she had escaped that particular torture, Coral knew that bound feet didn't hold the promise of happiness but, instead, the ugly specter of servitude and helplessness. She knew that whole feet, the feet her childhood friends laughed at and considered ugly, were the ticket to happiness, or at least a chance at it.

"Can you make a convincing belt of it?" Tiger asked.

"Yes, yes," Coral said, and began folding it in such a way that the Nu Shu embroidery was barely visible. "Not the height of fashion, but I think it will do."

"These men won't know the difference," Tiger said.

The noise rose louder in the street, the shouting and yelling and stomping of feet. They rushed to the window. As they watched, Professor Wong, who lived in the apartment above theirs, was dragged to the flames and tossed in, with little more effort than it took to dispense with an armload of books or an old Ming vase. He screamed, but was soon silenced by the flames.

"Oh, no," Coral wept. "I forgot about the old professor. Oh, how can they do that? How can the people cheer for this?"

"They don't know what they are doing," said Tiger. "None of them, the soldiers or the crowds. They are scared to go against what they think is the majority. And they get caught up in the frenzy."

"We must try to stop it."

More cheers rose from the crowd. People raised their small children to their shoulders so they could better see the spectacle of the burning man. Older children danced about and sang songs.

"I'm afraid it's too late for Professor Wong. And we can't

leave the apartment alone if we have any hope of protecting the Nu Shu. Besides, they warned us they would shoot if they saw anyone leaving. Compose yourself. They are still coming back. Remember? It will not do for you to look tear-streaked and agitated. We must appear as just two people with no stake in this, with nothing to hide. Get yourself quiet."

And with that the soldiers were back. They rapped loudly on the door and shouted as if drunk, whether with power or spirits one couldn't be sure. Coral and Tiger both took deep breaths and Tiger opened the door.

The men burst in and did, indeed, seem to be in a state of drunken frenzy.

"The last apartment of the day," Swift Wind shouted. "We found one good vase, Tiger, and that's about all. Which is good. Not too much to carry out to the fire. This whole building has yielded little. What have you got?"

With that, the men began to look under furniture and open drawers. Swift Wind checked the stove but skipped over the refrigerator. Coral dared not let her eyes meet Tiger's. The other soldier looked under the bed and sofa. "A couple extra pillows here," he shouted from the bedroom. "Want to take a nap?" he laughed. "Or toss them on the fire?"

"Just leave them," Swift Wind hollered. "That vase in the hall will fill your arms and I'd rather travel light."

"But what do these two people need four pillows for?"

"Forget it, will you?" Swift Wind answered. "Let's get out of here. Tiger, you turned into an old married man. I would never have predicted that. But I hope we did right by your little woman here. We'll never tell anyone that she has extra pillows under the bed. And that the bed is lumpy. Her reputation as an excellent housekeeper is still intact."

With that he let out a loud roar and his partner joined in the laugh.

"Let's get that vase into the fire before the flames go out," he ordered, and the two darted out the door, Swift Wind shooting a brief salute in Tiger's direction on his way.

As soon as the door was closed behind them Coral sank to the floor and began to weep. Tiger cradled her in his arms and offered what comfort he could.

"It's going to be all right now," he whispered. "They will not be back. And the Nu Shu is safe. We can keep it here now and when all this is over we can deliver it back to the women who did the embroidery, or to their families."

Coral sighed and wiped her eyes. But she was not convinced that the Nu Shu was saved forever. She could not know that already a professor at a university had found some Nu Shu and was studying it. That he would find a way to save the Nu Shu, but not for many years. Not until the turmoil in their country, in their beloved China, was settled down and the forces of destruction were quieted.

Tiger took her hand. "Read me a story, Coral. Read some Nu Shu to me."

So Coral stood up and retrieved a beautiful tablecloth from under the bed covers. Her hands trembled as she held it. This is what she read:

"I am making up songs and counting the fireflies. Each firefly flies away with a dream from my heart. The firefly will not live forever. I do not know which two hands will clap and put the firefly in between them. And I do not know which two hands will clap and kill my dreams. So I embroider my songs into this cloth. I cannot embroider the melody that I composed, but it does not matter. Whoever reads this can put her own melody into it because melody comes from the heart."

AFTERWORD

"The storyteller is deep inside every one of us.
The story-maker is always with us."
—Doris Lessing
Nobel Lecture, December 7, 2007

On a cool April morning in 1954, as the sun was just beginning to chase away the clouds of an early rain, an elderly woman, dressed in a simple brown coat and wearing no hat to cover her graying hair, stepped carefully down from a train platform in China. She looked around at what was the main street of a small village in the Jiangyong County of the Hunan Province. This was the village of her childhood, but it looked so different from those days that she recognized almost nothing of what she saw.

She'd left the village more than forty years earlier to marry the man her father had chosen for her. Her bound feet, at the time of her marriage, were quite tiny, just three inches in length. Many years into her marriage she had begun unwrapping them at night and leaving them unwrapped for longer and longer periods of time so that now her feet were considerably larger, though quite misshapen. Still, the fact that she had unwrapped her feet is what made this journey on her own, late in her life, possible.

Over the years the woman had communicated with some of her old friends, her "sworn sisters," on occasion, but in the last decade or so she had heard from no one. In all her married life she had never returned to the village where she had grown up because neither her husband nor her mother-in-law would permit it. Now her husband had died and his mother was dead also. Her oldest son, who now was the male family member who had responsibility for her, had given permission for her to visit her old home, and had even provided money for the train ticket and for purchasing food for the trip. She carried with her directions to her home, written long ago in Nu Shu, the women's script, but her vision was poor now and she was unable to make out the symbols clearly. She never expected that she would recognize so little of what she saw at the train station, that she would be so disoriented with regard to the location of the street that would take her to her old home.

The woman did remember that there was a police office right down the road from the train station, so she put her small bag under her arm and headed off in that direction, hoping that the location of the police had not changed in all the years she had been away. When she found it, the building seemed to have had a new addition built onto it, but it looked enough like the old building that she entered it with confidence and was not surprised to see two police officers sitting at desks inside.

The men were talking to each other, but stopped and looked at her when she approached their desks. They were respectful as she explained her plight, and she showed them the paper she carried with directions to her old family home. She'd written the directions herself many years ago when she thought she might forget them with age. She'd always hoped that the day would come when she would be allowed to see her old village again.

The officers looked long and hard at the paper, then at each other and then at the woman. The writing they were holding in their hands resembled Mandarin, but was more fluid, more design-like, less squared off. The symbols were completely unintelligible to them. The old woman knew the men were unlikely to understand the writing, but she didn't know what else to do with it.

"In what language is this written?" one of the men asked.

"It is the women's script," she answered. "That is the only language I know how to write."

. . . .

In my research I've encountered two different versions of this story and maybe there are more. In another telling the woman fainted on the train platform and was taken to the police station. I'd like to think she got there on her own but, really, it doesn't matter. What is important is that on that day a long-held secret was uncovered and the women of Hunan Province found their voice.

Still, it was decades before any attempt was made to translate the script and when that happened, it occurred in Taiwan rather than on the mainland. But the discovery launched an investigation that would ultimately lead to new directions in the study of women's place in Chinese history, the nature of alphabets and writing symbols, even a hint of espionage.

The directions the woman carried were, indeed, written in the "women's script," a writing system called Nu Shu which means, literally, women's writing. And this was, as she stated, the only language she knew how to write. This woman was one of the last few remaining women who could still read and write Nu Shu. She had learned to write and sew the forms from her mother and sisters, as had been the tradition for all the women in her village. And all through her married life she had nurtured her memory of the writing system by embroidering the Nu Shu onto tablecloths, fans, napkins, any household linens that could be decorated with needle and thread.

Throughout China's history, it was rare that a woman was allowed to go to school or to learn to write at home. In fact, as in most places in the world, historically, most men were not literate either. But it was in this particular county, Jiangyong, of Hunan Province, that women developed their own writing system and taught it to one another in secret. Who invented the writing method and why it started in this particular place, or when, is a matter for much speculation and all sorts of stories are told by way of explanation. Which, if any, of these stories is true is not known and may never be. What matters is that this woman and others learned the script because they were not allowed to attend school with their brothers and learn Mandarin. And they preserved the script for anywhere from two hundred to two thousand years – depending on which story you believe – because it afforded them a way to communicate with each other in writing when they could not visit in person.

When the script was discovered, there were few women left who knew how to read or write it because once the Communist regime took over the country, girls were sent to school where they studied side by side with the boys. So Nu Shu was quickly abandoned by the younger generation.

The woman at the police station had no idea of the part she was destined to play in the story of Nu Shu. She knew that she held in her hand a sample of women's writing, but to her it was just the script her friends and female relatives knew. A script kept away from the eyes of men as much as possible. It was writing, or more often needlework, that signified nothing of importance to men, but that was actually a form of expression that served to open a window into female life in pre-Communist China and give a voice to women whose own, male-dominated culture conspired to keep them silent.

The police who first viewed the Nu Shu writing were completely mystified by it. The idea that this old peasant woman knew a language they had never seen was not something they could comprehend. One of the theories they came up with by way of explanation was that this was some sort of secret military code and that the woman was involved in espionage. Though far-fetched, it was a fortunate idea because it kept the writing under scrutiny for some time. The paper was eventually turned over to Professor Gong Zhe-bing of Central Southern Ethnic Studies College in Wuban, China, who interviewed the woman and began to study the script.

Gong developed quite a relationship with the woman, even having her stay at his home (where she claimed she saw a flush toilet for the first time), and he became convinced that Nu Shu was a legitimate writing system. The predominant thinking at the time was that for a language to be legitimate it had to be understood by all members of society. Since Nu Shu was known only to women, the logic went, it could not be considered a legitimate language. Gong was a lone voice for quite some time in recognizing the importance of Nu Shu.

It was not until 1986 that a home was found for Nu Shu, ironically in Taiwan. On that island martial law was being lifted at that time and people were being allowed to meet freely in groups. An organization which had existed since 1982 under the cover of being a magazine publishing company was now out in the open as the first feminist organization in Taiwan. Gong approached this group, called The Awakening Foundation (officially established as a feminist organization in 1987) with the Nu Shu writing that he had collected with the help of the old woman and some of her friends who knew the script. He was looking for help in translating the language into Mandarin, or Nan Shu, men's writing. No organization on mainland China was interested at that point.

The Awakening Foundation greeted this project with enormous enthusiasm. Gong provided three women from China, all in their late eighties by then, who knew how to write the script, to help in the translation process. The Awakening Foundation gathered together thirty female Taiwanese volunteers from all walks of life to work with the Chinese women. In six months they had translated enough material to publish a book, which was released in 1991. The book, written in Mandarin and named Nu Shu, contains the story of the discovery of Nu Shu, and translations of some of the stories and poems into Mandarin, printed side-by-side with the original Nu Shu.

This material, mostly recorded on table linens, fans, handkerchiefs, cloths used to bind little girls' feet, and more items that have been found since the publication of the Awakening Foundation's book, is important for more than just its literary value. Read as a whole, it forms a report on the life of women inside the family in this part of China, recorded by the women themselves rather than by professional historians. It adds enormously to the historical material that already exists regarding family life in China. It presents the female perspective on foot-binding, arranged marriages, female friendship, and other aspects of pre-Communist Chinese culture, written by women for their sisters, mothers and friends, rather than for an official historical record.

We may never know the answer to one big question: How did a group of women, denied the right to an education, develop a way of communicating in a writing system more efficient than the official language of their nation? Frequently men dismissed the whole idea that their wives had a written language because when they would ask what a particular symbol meant the women could not answer the question. Nu Shu differs from Nan Shu in that instead of having some 50,000 characters, each representing a different word, it has approximately 1,500 characters, syllabic in nature, each having a different meaning depending upon where in a sentence it appears. With the knowledge of as few as 300 characters a woman could communicate quite adequately in Nu Shu.

Nu Shu was discovered by accident and preserved by luck. It fell out of use because women didn't need it anymore. And the leaders of the Cultural Revolution, who wanted to destroy all "art of the old," saw the beautiful Nu Shu embroidery as part of that art. They burned every piece of it they could find, which almost caused its demise in the mid-twentieth century. Although many artifacts were lost in local riots, Nu Shu did not disappear entirely and it remains a legacy of the women of this place. It stands as a testament to the determination to be heard, to have one's story told. It gives a voice to women who had much to say but no power to be heard in their lifetime. And those of the Cultural Revolution who called it art were correct. It is, indeed, art, not only in the literary sense in which all writing is art, but in the visual meaning of the word. The symbols themselves are beautiful and the decorated linens and fans are exquisite expressions of the meaning and emotion of life.

. . . .

Generally a work of fiction carries a disclaimer at the front of the book stating that any resemblance to real persons or places is purely coincidental. This book carries no such statement. Although the story is fiction, it is based on translations of original Nu Shu writing and thus the characters do resemble real people – the recorders of these stories in the Nu Shu script. Sadly, we do not know the identities of the women whose writings survived and form the inspiration for this story. My fervent hope is that, if only to a small degree, their stories will become known through this book. And their voices, systematically silenced for so many years, will at last be heard.

—Norma Libman

December 2013

SEWING THE STORY

Mandarin	Nu Shu
耐 Patience	
静 Silence	
現 Emergence	

Based on drawings and translations from Nu Shu
(The Awakening Foundation) and The Tao of Women
(Humanics Trade)

Notice the simplicity of the Nu Shu compared with the complicated Mandarin symbols. Economy of design was necessary for a number of reasons. Nu Shu was often produced under duress and always in secret. Women sewed alone or together in groups, but never with men present. On some occasions it was written but it was almost always sewn so if the women were observed it would look like they were just decorating household linens – in other words, doing women's work.

All the symbols had to be committed to memory. To aid in memorization, the symbols often resembled shapes found in nature or the action they stood for. The Nu Shu symbol for "emergence," for instance, seems to leap off the page as compared to the heavy Mandarin symbol for the same idea.

ACKNOWLEDGEMENTS

First, I'd like to thank the woman or women of Hunan Province in China who invented the Nu Shu script. And all the women who learned it and taught it to their daughters for an unknown number of generations. I wrote this book because I believe their stories should continue to be heard, should not be lost now that the Nu Shu is no longer needed.

I want to thank Su Chien-ling for teaching me so much about the culture of China, and her team at the Awakening Foundation in Taipei, Taiwan, who translated the Nu Shu into Mandarin. I am especially indebted to the four people who translated various portions of available Nu Shu text from the Mandarin into English for me. They are Ching Bezine, William W. Chiang, Jian Hua Guo and Grace Hsu.

I am grateful to my writer friends who listened to all or parts of the book at various times, sometimes more than once, and made insightful comments and cheered me on. Thank you Gwenellen Janov, Joy Price, Phyllis Skoy, Mary Stuever, Karen Crane, Jessica Gordon, Joan Jander, Daisy Kates and Beverly Ledbetter.

Technical assistance of various types was provided by Gary Priester and Mary Carter. Where would I be without you?

My children and grandchildren have already been mentioned

at the front of the book, but I'll say here that they are the loves of my life and there would be no point to writing at all if not for them.

And last, I want to thank three people without whose wisdom, sage advice and persistent encouragement this book would still be just a stack of papers on my desk: Ann Paden, Harry Guffee and Francis Roe. Thank you. Thank you. Thank you.

GLOSSARY

Cultural Revolution. 1966–1976. A social-political movement in the People's Republic of China, which was a policy of Mao Zedong intending to cement the philosophy of socialism by removing – by violent means where necessary – all capitalist, traditional, and ancient cultural and intellectual elements from Chinese society. The Red Guard, composed of the military, urban workers, various youths, and Communist Party leaders roamed the country harassing citizens, seizing property thought to be historic artifacts, and ransacking cultural and religious sites.

Foot Binding. A tradition, possibly lasting as long as one thousand years in China, in which very young girls – sometimes as young as six years of age – had their feet bound until the bones were broken. The mother performed this duty. The ideal bound foot was between three and five inches in length and the sole of the foot, when properly bound, resembled a lotus flower. Bound feet kept women subservient to men as they could not walk far on their own. It also gave the women a gait that men in this culture considered sexy. The small, broken foot could be used for various sexual practices. Prostitutes with beautifully bound feet were in demand and families of young girls with ideal feet were able to secure good marriages for them. The practice was outlawed in 1911 but it took many years for word of the new law to reach the most remote of the villages.

Hunan Province. A province in southeastern China, just south of the middle portion of the Yangtze River and south of Lake Dongting. The Xiang River runs through the province. It is known for the embroidery skills of its residents, who are ninety percent Han ethnic. It is the only province in China where Nu Shu writing has been found.

Jiangyong County. The county within Hunan Province where the Nu Shu culture flourished. It is believed the script stayed in that area because the mountainous terrain and the women's bound feet made foot travel out of the area difficult.

Mandarin. The official standard spoken language of China.

Marriage Cry. A ritual engaged in by a group of sworn sisters, who had learned Nu Shu and household arts together, before the marriage of one of the members. The girls (generally in their early teens) would sing songs and cry for three days, bemoaning the loss of their closest friends as they prepared to be taken to the home of their bridegroom, whom they usually did not know. The sorrow was genuine as this was a permanent rupture in the most meaningful relationship in their young lives.

Nan Shu. Men's writing. Official writing.

Nu Shu. Women's writing. Actually a writing system, developed at an unknown time by an unknown woman or women as a means of communication among women, who were not formally educated and, therefore, did not learn Nan Shu.

Sworn Sisterhood. A group of girls with favorable birth

signs, ideally around seven in number. They would grow up together, in a very close relationship, learning how to be good wives and daughters-in-law when the time for marriage came. They learned Nu Shu together, each one resting her hand upon the hand of the older sister, mother, grandmother or cousin who was teaching the secret script. This helped to foster a very close friendship among the girls. In fact, for most women, the relationship with their sworn sisters was the closest relationship they would have in their lives.

Taiping Rebellion. 1850-1864. A religious/political movement that brought Christian ideas into China and attempted to bring down the Ching dynasty. An excerpt of Nu Shu text has been found that describes the Taiping Rebellion. There is also a coin produced during the rebellion that has Nu Shu script on it. This indicates Nu Shu existed at least as far back as the mid-nineteenth century.

Tea Girl. This can refer to a girl who serves tea in a tea room, but at times it has also meant prostitute. The reference in Nu Shu samples seem to suggest prostitute, but I did not encounter the term in any writing that I could date.

Third Day Book. A book presented to a bride on the third day after her wedding when she returned home to await confirmation of pregnancy and sometimes to stay until it was time for the baby to be born. The book, written in the Nu Shu script by the bride's mother, tells the girl how to behave as a wife and encourages her not to be depressed about her situation. The covers were red, the color of happiness in China, but the books are not congratulatory. They are more accurately described as educational and sympathetic. The books contained blank pages for the bride to write about herself in Nu Shu.

Wedding Sing. The singing of sorrowful songs by the members of a girl's sworn sisterhood at her wedding.

BIBLIOGRAPHY

The following contributed to my understanding of the Nu Shu writing system and the culture of China, particularly the practice of foot binding. It is by no means a comprehensive list of sources, but would make a good start for anyone who wants to read more about this subject. In addition to the sources listed here it should also be noted that my conversation with Su Chien-ling of the Awakening Foundation in 1994 in Taipei, Taiwan, started me on my research and resulted in an article written by me and published in the Chicago Tribune on May 22, 1994.

—N.L.

Bjorksten, Johan. *Learning to Write Chinese Characters*. New Haven: Yale University Press, 1994.

Bo, Shi. *Between Heaven and Earth: A History of Chinese Writing*. Boston and London: Shambhala, 2003.

Chang, Jung. *Wild Swans: Three Daughters of China*. New York: Anchor Books, 1991.

Chang, Pang-Mei Natasha. *Bound Feet and Western Dress*. New York: Anchor Books, 1997.

Chang, Raymond and Margaret Scrogin Chang. *Speaking Chinese: A Cultural History of the Chinese Language.* New York: W.W. Norton and Company, 2001.

Chiang, William W. *"We Two Know the Script; We Have Become Good Friends": Linguistic and Social Aspects of The Women's Script Literacy in Southern Hunan, China.* Lanham, Maryland: University Press of America, 1995.

Go, Ping-gam. *What Character is That?* Larkspur, CA: Simplex Publications, 1995.

Gordon, Cyrus H. *Forgotten Scripts: Their Ongoing Discovery and Decipherment.* New York: Barnes and Noble, Inc. and Basic Books, Inc., 1982.

Ho, Cindy. *Trailing the Written Word: The Art of Writing Among China's Ethnic Minorities.* Catalog of the John Jay College Gallery Exhibition, New York, November 3 to 28, 1997.

Lindqvist, Cecilia. *China: Empire of Living Symbols.* Reading, MA: Addison-Wesley Publishing Company, Inc. 1989.

McLaren, Anne E. *"Crossing Gender Boundaries in China: Nushu Narratives."* www.sshe.murdoch.edu.au/intersection/back_issues/nushu2.html.

Metz, Pamela K. and Jacqueline L. Tobin. *The Tao of Women.* Atlanta: Humanics Trade, 1995.

Nu Shu. Publication of the Awakening Foundation. Taipei, Taiwan, 1991. (Translations of Nu Shu to Mandarin).

Ping, Wang. *Aching for Beauty: Footbinding in China.* New York: Anchor Books, 2000.

Roberts, J.A.G. *A Concise History of China*. Cambridge: Harvard University Press, 2000.

Silber, Cathy. "*From Daughter to Daughter-in-Law in the Women's Script of Southern Hunan*." In Engendering China: Women, Culture, and the State. Edited by Gilmatrin, Christina K., et.al. 47-68. Harvard Contemporary China Series. No. 10. Cambridge: Harvard University Press. 1994.

Xinran. *The Good Women of China: Hidden Voices*. New York: Pantheon Books, 2002.

Zhao, Liming. "Nushu: Chinese Women's Characters." *International Journal of the Sociology of Language*. 129:127-137.

FICTION

Hahn, Kimiko. *Mosquito and Ant*. New York: W.W. Norton and Company, 1999. (Poetry)

Harrison, Kathryn. *The Binding Chair*. New York: Perennial, 2000.

Schoppa, Keith R. *Song Full of Tears: Nine Centuries of Chinese Life at Xiang Lake*. New Haven: Yale University Press, 2005.

See, Lisa. *Snow Flower and the Secret Fan*. New York: Random House, 2005